The Magnificent Moustache

and other stories

The Magnificent Moustache and other stories

Published by The Conrad Press Ltd. in the United Kingdom 2022

Tel: +44(0)1227 472 874
www.theconradpress.com
info@theconradpress.com

ISBN 978-1-914913-85-3

Copyright © Jenny Sanders, 2022

Printed and bound in Great Britain by Clays Ltd, Elcograf S.p.A

Typesetting and cover design by The Book Typesetters
www.thebooktypesetters.com

Cover and internal illustrations by Amanda Young
www.yong9jy.wixsite.com/mysite

The Conrad Press logo was designed by Maria Priestley.

The Magnificent Moustache

and other stories

Jenny Sanders

To my children:
Kirsty, Elspeth, Rhiannon
and Callum
for whom I first wrote these stories,
and for everyone who is still
a child at heart.

Contents

The Magnificent Moustache

The Magnificent Moustache

Lord Clanville-Smythe, 7th Viscount of Perrimead-on-the-Wold, was not to be disturbed. He sat in his personal deck chair that was trimmed with African leather and placed in the sunshine on the North lawn. His pocket watch was lying beside him on a small table next to his glasses and a book (which he had no intention of reading but which he felt looked earnest), and with a newspaper over his hairy face.

He was snoring; loudly. It was not a lordly thing to do but he had had sinus trouble as a young boy and had learnt to live with the inconvenience of a snore. Truth to tell, it bothered him significantly less than it bothered his wife who had spent many a night tucked up in the peace and serenity of the spare room leaving him to huff, puff, snorkel and snarl to his heart's content in the main bedroom.

Also, to be strictly honest, he could not really be said to be sitting on the chair; having been asleep for at least the past half hour he had sunk down into a slouching, half-lying position which meant he would be stiff and grumpy when he woke up.

Now you may think I have been very rude to say that this titled gentleman had a hairy face. Not at all. Not one bit. It was a source of great pride to Lord Clanville-Smythe that his hair grew at a really terrific rate, but a source of great discomfort to his long-suffering wife. It grew on his arms; it grew on his legs, it grew on his chest, on his head and most certainly it grew on his face. That is not to say that he never shaved – although, strictly speaking it was his barber, Giles Thatcher, who had that dubious honour.

No, no; the 7th Viscount of Perrimead-on-the-Wold was most particular about his facial hair and personal grooming, and was the proud owner of a much-admired beard and a truly extraordinary moustache. Every morning, he not only smoothed his beard as any whiskered gentleman might do, but he combed his moustache with the tender strokes of one handling ancient parchment. He had a fine-toothed, cedar-wood comb that he had had made especially for the purpose and which, he was assured, would keep the moths at bay. The thought of moths nesting in his moustache gave him the shivers and motivated him to give each flamboyant twirl a regulation 100 strokes a day. Every second Tuesday for the past twenty years he also had it oiled and trimmed to keep it in perfect shape.

This afternoon he awoke from his nap with a jolt when the cat, who had been stalking mice in the shrubbery and noticed his somnolence, decided to shatter the peace by jumping straight onto the newspaper, and therefore onto his face. In his fright, the Viscount leapt from his chair with an impressive athleticism, scattering newspaper pages every which way, which frightened the cat almost as much as she had planned to disturb her master.

'Good gracious Tilly!' spluttered Lord Clanville-Smythe. 'Whatever do you think you're doing?' His face was turning an alarming shade of purple and small bubbles of spit appeared to be let loose into the air as he shook himself back to unwelcome consciousness. It was not a pleasant sight.

Tilly, not surprisingly, had nothing to say and walked off loftily to investigate some strange rustlings she'd heard in the rhubarb, just as Lady Clanville-Smythe appeared with the tea tray and a folding chair for herself. Her husband perked up considerably at the sight of food, especially the plate bearing slices of Battenburg cake which had been his favourite since childhood. He liked the order and symmetry of the yellow and pink squares; they reassured him that neatness and precision were still functioning in his household, not just in his moustache.

With the dexterity of a much-practised multi-tasker, his wife hooked the small table closer with her foot, set down the tray, arranged the wobbly folding chair for herself and prepared to pour the tea.

'Do pick up the newspaper, Gerald,' she scolded, 'it really shouldn't be blowing all over the garden.'

There was a muttering, and mumbling which she hoped might be a well-disguised apology – it wasn't – as he laboriously fetched the stray pages and sat down again with great effort and an enormous grunt, by which time she had poured the tea, added the sugar cubes, stirred the hot liquid to perfection and taken a welcome bite of a cucumber sandwich.

The 7th Viscount of Perrimead-on-the-Wold took a deep breath and reached automatically for a slice of cake, but the peace was immediately shattered by a throaty exclamation.

'Good heavens Fenella!' The cake tumbled unheeded to the grass beside him. Lady Clanville-Smythe was immediately alarmed.

'What is it, Gerald?' she asked with some anxiety. 'Are you quite well?'

'Well? Of course I'm well. But here, look at this. Look at *this*!' He thrust the newspaper towards her with such energy that the rest of the cake followed the first unfortunate slice.

'Oh Gerald, I do wish you'd be careful,' she scolded again, 'I don't know what's got into you.'

'Well, blazes woman! Look! Read!'

The baffled lady obediently took the newspaper which was now scrunched up into a fairly unreadable bunch of creases and folds. She put on her glasses, which were so conveniently dangling on a chain around her neck, and peered at what was left of the publication while her husband clicked his tongue impatiently.

'My dear…' she began, 'I really have no idea…'

'Good golly!' he exclaimed testily, snatching the paper back again and dislodging sandwiches indiscriminately as he pointed to something on the bottom corner of the page. 'There! Right there!'

Lady Clanville-Smythe obediently lent forwards to see what it was that had so gripped the attention of her blustering husband. Sure enough, there was an advertisement, or rather an announcement, and this is what it said:

You are invited to the **annual**

Perrimead-on-the-Wold

COUNTY FÊTE, FAYRE & CARNIVAL

First Saturday in May 10am – 4pm

Showcasing the best of breed for cattle, sheep and pigs

Home-made cake competition

Fruit and vegetable display – prizes for best in show
(largest and most unusual)

Dog show

Flower show

Horse rides

Merry-go-round & Thrilling Entertainments

Refreshments

Baton Twirling from the
Upper-Brightwell County Champions

First National Moustache Competition

Tickets on sale at the gate

Prizes to be awarded 3.30pm

Enter all competitions
following the details below…

'Oooh, is it that time again already?' she murmured, 'I must look out my grandmother's treacle cake recipe.'

'Treacle be blowed!' puffed the Viscount. 'See this other competition! My moustache will finally get the recognition it deserves!'

With that he hauled himself out of his deckchair again and hurried back to the house to attend to grooming his pride and joy for the second time that day.

The Viscountess sighed resignedly as she quickly gathered up the debris of the ruined cake and sandwiches, brushed the crumbs off her ample chest and took the tray back to the house before sitting down with a family book of recipes for the rest of the evening.

There then began a rota of preparations that would make your eyes simply water. While cake-making is quite a straightforward kind of business, Lady Clanville-Smythe took a few practice runs at the treacle cake of yesteryear, not because she needed to improve her technique in any way at all – indeed she was a former county champion in this category – but because she enjoyed a generous slice herself, and also because it gave her something to do while her husband became increasingly obsessed with his facial hair. So, she was either in the kitchen or ambling round her garden which was *her* pride and joy and a great deal less demanding than her husband's toilette. A little light weeding, strategic planting, pruning and planning kept her busy and content, so long as it wasn't raining or too cold.

The 7th Viscount of Perrimead-on-the-Wold however, had far more ambitious aspirations and preparations on his schedule. Without further ado, he made daily appointments with Giles Thatcher at his *Salon Of Exclusive Male Grooming*, where he was pampered, pinched and preened with the care of a consummate professional.

Mr. Thatcher carefully concocted balms and balsams, ointments and unguents, lotions and liniments, butters and beeswax, polish and pomades, using exotic ingredients all designed to improve the growth, quality and texture of the fabulous face furniture. He brushed it, combed it, sang to it, soaked it and teased it into fantastic shapes before waxing the ends to a sharp point, and finally measuring it every day. The results were plotted on a graph he had made for this exact purpose. Together the men clasped their hands in glee at the prospect of what might be. Surely there could not be a greater, more impressive, more glorious moustache in the entire country!

Already Lord Clanville-Smythe could see himself not only winning the prize, but gracefully acknowledging admiring crowds, receiving plaudits and accolades from the great and the good, perhaps enjoying national, or even international recognition for his truly marvellous moustache. His eyes shone at the very thought of it all. And all the time his moustache grew and grew.

For two weeks he barely slept, he was so excited. On one moonlit night, he even ventured out into his wife's greenhouse and anointed himself with a few drops of her liquid fertiliser, hoping it would give him the final growth boost he wanted, to ensure the championship would be his.

I don't know whether it was the skill of Mr. Thatcher or the visit to the greenhouse, but with just one week until the day of the County Fayre, that moustache was blooming. Blooming enormous! In fact, it had become quite a nuisance.

If the Viscount turned around too fast he started sweeping ornaments off shelves and onto the floor. Several family heirlooms were destroyed beyond repair in this clumsy way. He had to go into rooms sideways now to avoid squashing the moustache on the way through, and he kept leaving all the doors open for fear of closing them on it. More than once, he was perilously close to poking his wife in the eye and had resorted to blowing her kisses from some distance away. It was most unsatisfactory.

When he fell asleep in his garden chair and started to snore, birds began to perch in it, even though the whole hairy thing vibrated alarmingly. Tilly, of course, found this new turn of events irresistible. She was frequently caught attempting to pounce on the birds who were, inevitably, always far too quick for her. Instead she resorted to batting at the hairy protuberance with her paws; twice she scratched him across the cheek causing him to wake up with a roar, startled and confused.

Bedtime was definitely not a good time for the moustache, which now extended a good ten inches either side of the Viscount's nose. This meant that he had to sleep flat on his back for fear of bending it, or crushing it, every time he turned over (a sure sign of a night of raucous snoring to come). He slept with hairbrushes either side of his head to stop this eventuality and, consequently, his wife took refuge more permanently in the spare room, shaking her head over the ludicrous way in which his facial hair had now taken over their entire lives. She had been compelled to make a special fabric cover for it, which tied up behind his head like a surgeon's mask, so that the moustache could be protected from stray crumbs, hot soup, flailing noodles and other food debris. It had been a labour of love, for she did indeed love her husband dearly in spite of his many foibles; but she found his infatuation with the wretched thing really quite exasperating.

It was now two days before the county Fayre, and Lady Clanville-Smythe had brought all the ingredients to make her trusty cake, which she planned to cook the evening before. That way it would have time to cool but not to dry out. She set aside a favourite tin to transport it intact to the venue, and then wondered what to do next.

The smell of the latest moustache oil was particularly penetrating today which made being in the house uncomfortable. Gerald had changed his lubricant from a fairly pleasant citrus extract to a woody elixir which reminded her of damp compost – something she could smell outside anyway and where at least the fresh air made it bearable.

Thinking of her garden, she reviewed her tasks: she had already planted her tomatoes and watered the hanging baskets. Her shed needed painting, as did the bird house, but with evening drawing in that was clearly a job for another day.

Instead, she pulled on her gauntlets and set off to the rose garden armed with a pair of secateurs for some brisk pruning, and perhaps to find some blooms to put in a vase. The white roses were especially good this year; she loved their fragrance and the spare room could use a more personal touch.

It was there that the Viscount found her some time later as dusk was falling. He was just back from his latest salon appointment, and keen to let her know that Giles' graph had had to be extended, since the magnificent moustache had now grown another incredible half an inch each side in the last week.

'Isn't it marvellous?' he asked her, basking in the glory of his assured victory.

'Of course it is, dear,' she answered automatically, peering through the dying light as she leaned across three plants to sever the head of a particularly sad looking, brown-edged rose and toss it into the basket at her feet.

'Tut!' She clicked her tongue several times. 'Tut; I do believe that might be an aphid. Oh dear; that will never do. I can't have my roses ruined by pests.'

'Where?' asked the Viscount feigning interest in an effort to stir her to more enthusiasm about his latest growth report.

'Why, just there, Gerald. On that leaf under the wilting Tranquility Rose.'

It was unfortunate that she chose that precise moment to snip the head off another drooping rose because her husband chose the exact same moment to lean further in to see the troublesome insect for himself. There was a snip; a gasp; a terrible moment of silence, and then a bellow and a wail of such intensity that the sound bounced off the garden wall and caused Tilly to seek refuge beneath the rhododendrons.

The 7th Viscount of Perrimead-on-the-Wold ran up the garden with an admirable turn of speed, clutching his face and fearing the worst. The 7th Viscountess meanwhile, dropped her secateurs, clapped her hand over her mouth and trembled violently. What on earth had she done? Had she

really just stabbed her husband in the face with a gardening implement? The horror! She would never forgive herself.

In fear and trepidation she followed her husband, at a more respectable pace, back into the house where she found him on the bathroom floor, crouched over a hand mirror and rocking back and forth, moaning in undisguised distress. Cautiously, she ventured over the threshold.

'Oh my darling; I'm so sorry. Did I cut you? Are you bleeding? Let me get some ice… or some cloths.'

Her husband only whimpered.

'Oh Gerald, I'm so terribly sorry.' The poor lady's eyes brimmed with tears of regret. 'The blade was quite sharp, I know. I wouldn't scar you for the world, darling one.'

Lord Clanville-Smythe was not feeling very lordly at that moment. In fact he was feeling supremely sorry for himself as he reluctantly lifted his head from his knees and turned slowly towards her. She gasped again, and was mightily relieved to see that there was no blood, but most assuredly, there was almost no moustache either. One half of it was completely gone. Sheared clean off. Vanished.

If she had not felt so guilty, I think Lady Clanville-Smythe might almost have ventured a laugh, which would definitely not have been the best thing at that moment, so it was probably prudent that she didn't. Her husband's moustache now looked so lop-sided it was comical, but his face wore a dejected expression of such utter defeat, heart-rending loss and woe, that her own heart was torn in two.

It need hardly be said that there were tears on both sides; some ugly words on one (I'm sure you can guess the source of those unpleasant words, but I shall forbear to enlighten you here), and many hours of searching for the right words of comfort. Alas, they were not to be found. The marvellous moustache was no more.

With less than 24 hours to go before the County Fayre, there was a grim determination in the eye of the 7th Viscount as he made his way to the premises of Giles Thatcher the next morning, wearing a scarf over his nose and mouth, and clasping a small paper bag. In it was the amputated facial hair, retrieved from the flower bed and looking more like a very sick vole than a splendid, competition-winning moustache. Mr. Thatcher swiftly drew the blinds and closed the shutters so that prying eyes were denied the sorry sight of the cloven hair.

The story was told in detail, and quite possibly with some exaggeration, but in the circumstances perhaps you might think it understandable and overlook it this once.

Now the question was only: what could be done? Did Mr. Thatcher have some magic glue that could fix the problem? He did not; although he tried for almost two hours. The hair didn't sit right; the angle was wrong; you could see the join, and the whole thing was an awkward mess.

Would it be possible to substitute something else…? A stick of liquorice perhaps? Some silly string teased into shape? Sheep's wool? Something from the theatrical make-up box might be worth exploring? For the next few hours they both racked their brains and then racked each others' brains, and buckled down to try some of their desperate suggestions, even the crazy ones involving worms and slugs – a slimy and unsatisfactory endeavour.

Far into the night, they experimented. Giles Thatcher called on his years of experience and all the tricks of his craft, but even he was flummoxed. He rolled up his sleeves and sweated as he laboured to create a moustache that could come close to the one he had nurtured for his client with such devotion for so many years.

He constructed elaborate replacements made of *papier-mâché*, pipe-cleaners and pasta, felt and fur, yarn and yoghurt, silk and sacking, charcoal and cheese (the one wrapped in black wax); but try as he might, nothing could come close to the original. Some were too scratchy, some were the wrong colour or didn't match in texture; some disintegrated when the Viscount sneezed and the yoghurt simply slipped right off.

Lord Clanville-Smythe bore it all stoically, pursing his lips every now and again as he took another deep breath and forced himself to gaze upon the ruin that now ran across his upper lip, looking in the mirror and bravely holding back tears of despair. Finally, with a gulp and a sob, together they faced the inevitable and unpalatable truth.

Under the cover of darkness Lord Clanville-Smythe slunk home in the shadows carrying the sorry and slightly heavier bag of facial hair. There he retreated to the sanctuary of the kitchen, where the smell of the freshly made treacle cake his wife had prepared still hung in the air. He was there for some considerable time before making his way slowly up the stairs to his bed for a few hours of reflection and restless sleep.

He did not emerge the next morning and Lady Clanville-Smythe thought it best to leave him alone to mourn the loss of his pride and joy, as well as the loss of the now dead dream of winning the first ever National Moustache Competition. She knew all too well that he would be devastated and she, contrite as she was, had no words to comfort him though she knew in her heart that it had merely been a terrible, ghastly accident.

While she admitted to herself that there had been times when she would gladly have severed the infuriating thing and returned to the comfort of their bedroom, she knew it was nothing more than a passing fancy, an idle wish, for – as you know – she was very fond of her hairy husband.

There was still no sign of Lord Clanville-Smythe at breakfast, and in spite of knocking gently on his door and whispering through the keyhole, he neither responded nor appeared. With a heavy heart the Viscountess took her cake – now nestled in a cloth in the tin she had especially chosen – and popped it into a capacious shopping bag before making her way to the Fayre alone.

She left the treacle treat on display in a large marquee amongst Victoria sponges and chocolate gateaux, and went to investigate the other stalls and entertainments. She admired massive marrows and bulbous beetroot, colossal cauliflowers and beautiful broccoli. She stared at strange artichokes and giant squashes, and enjoyed the riot of colours and heady fragrances of the flower show. There were rows of hay bales stacked up to make pens to accommodate the best-of-breed show, which were now occupied by the cleanest pigs and most pampered sheep she had ever seen. There were huge muscular bulls, and cows with liquid eyes and beautiful long lashes that blinked at her slowly in the spring sunshine.

The dog show was clearly popular: all shapes and sizes of dog were there, wagging tails and licking faces for sheer joy. One Collie dog navigated the obstacle course with incredible speed; a Labrador jumped over logs like an Olympic hurdler while a wire-haired Terrier, to the delight of the crowd, ignored them all and made a beeline for the ice-cream van instead. People laughed and pointed, shouted, whistled and whooped, waving their candy floss and cornets; they were having a grand old time enhanced by the fairground rides and sugary snacks.

The Upper-Brightwell Baton Twirlers were a triumph; their uniforms a wonder of tailoring and fringing, the sunlight lighting up the brass buttons like golden toffees. Such a stomping of white leather boots, such a whirling and twiddling of the famous wands – so fast the human eye could barely keep up with them – had never before been seen at the County Showground. The girls threw them high in the air while they pirouetted, hopped and jumped, catching them dextrously like the county champions they were. The crowd was enchanted and both their excitement and their cheers crescendoed. (The following week, several small children could have been observed in their various back gardens, inspired to attempt the same moves with ordinary sticks: new champions in the making perhaps...)

It was a shame Gerald had not come with her. Lady Clanville-Smythe remembered a time thirty years before when they had enjoyed riding the bumper cars and the big wheel together. She didn't have the heart to ride alone and regretted quite bitterly the accident in the rose garden. Still, what was done was done; she did not know how she could put things right.

Blowing her nose loudly with a lavender-scented handkerchief from her handbag, she took a deep breath and made her lonesome way to the main stage for the final events of the Fayre. At least there would be treacle cake for tea today; it was a comforting thought.

But first, there were rosettes for the livestock, certificates for the fruit, vegetable and flower winners, and a shiny cup for the athletic Collie dog and his owner. Then, the last extravaganza of the day before the final cake prize-giving (an old tradition that persisted for no logical reason): the first ever National Moustache Competition. This was announced by a trumpet blast over the tannoy which worked effectively to attract the attention of those now thinking of turning their weary feet towards home.

A row of thirty gentlemen filed onto the stage

and stood with their backs to the crowd; all but one (competitor 3, who had actually planned a quiet day of fishing today before discovering that his wife had entered his name without telling him and, consequently, was not a happy man) believed it was their time to shine. It was certainly a novelty and one cheeky wag called out, 'Is this the knobbly knees competition then?' People laughed and called out encouragement as they began jostling further forward to see what it was all about.

'Competitor 1!' called the disembodied voice from the loudspeakers.

The first man turned with a flourish to face the crowd, who all said, 'Oooooh!' He was sporting a thin moustache which had grown around his upper lip and hung down below his chin like left-over spaghetti.

'Competitor 2!' The next man turned to show off a bushy moustache which tumbled into a beard and grew to half way down his chest. 'Ahhhhhh!'

breathed the crowd admiringly; this was more like it.

'Competitor 3!' This moustache was a strange and straggly affair which had no chance of winning. 'Euuughgh!' responded the crowd, rather rudely, because of course this was the poor chap who hadn't intended to be here at all. He only had a moustache because he worked nights and didn't like to wake his family with the sound of shaving just as they were all going to sleep, so only shaved at weekends, which was actually very thoughtful of him.

'Competitor 4!' Another moustache; this time jet-black and curled like those you might see in old Italian portraits.

'Competitor 5!' ... so it went on.

Each moustache – and there was a great variety: long, thick, dyed (one fellow sported all the colours of the rainbow in his), handlebar, horseshoe, pencil, walrus, chevron, plaited, curled, scalloped, toothbrush – was greeted with a

cacophony of crowd sounds: some appreciative, some not.

Lady Clanville-Smythe sighed; she could hardly bear to watch. How she wished Gerald could have been there with his handlebar waxed wonder; he would have outshone them all. She had no doubt now that, impressive as some of these were, he would have been the easy winner. Although she had not enjoyed the moustache or its consequences – breaking things, poking her, annoying Tilly, taking so much time, effort and attention etc – she also knew that for him it had been more than a hobby; it was something very precious and she was heart-broken that it was she, of all people, who had inadvertently thwarted his moment of triumph. She should have been his biggest cheer-leader.

Miserably turning away, she made her way through the throng; she couldn't bear to see someone else take the prize which she knew was rightfully her husband's.

Thus it was that she was on the very edge of the crowd when one Mr Arnold Pertwee was hailed as the first National Moustache Champion; competitor 7 had nailed it in the face – literally – of some stiff competition from numbers 12 and 27. It was what it was.

With a sigh, she turned her face to home just as the voice from the tannoy announced: 'And finally, ladies and gentlemen, boys and girls, we are pleased to announce this year's home-made cake winners.'

In her reverie, the Viscountess had almost forgotten about the cakes. Truly, she would rather go home, brew a cup of tea, make do with a biscuit instead and forget all about it; but she knew her duty. Taking another deep breath and blowing her nose once more, she stepped back as a man in a long raincoat elbowed her aside without apology, accidentally stepping on her foot in his own hurry to get to the front. *Dear me; how rude,* she thought, as with a few 'Excuse me's of her own, she found herself a place with a view of the stage to see and hear the results.

'I give you this year's Perrimead-on-the-Wold County Cake champions!' announced the voice dramatically. There was another trumpet flourish. Everyone leant forward expectantly.

'In third place, with a luscious Lemon Drizzle cake...' (more trumpeting) '...Mrs Ethel Meddleweed!'

A ripple of appreciative applause ran through the crowd as the cake was promenaded across the stage under a glass dome by a uniformed girl, who reunited it with its maker. Third prize was a large bouquet of flowers and a yellow rosette presented by the same girl. Mrs Meddleweed's face went red with pleasure as she disappeared behind the blooms.

'In second place, an annual favourite and former

Champion…' (even more trumpeting) '… Lady Clanville-Smythe's excellent and terrific Teatime Treacle Cake!'

It was true; everyone loved this cake, and it had won her first prize several years in a row before people started watching so many baking shows on television and honing their own cake-making skills. Still, second place was not to be sneezed at and, after quickly blowing her nose for the final time, the Viscountess made her way carefully through the clapping crowd to the stage where another uniformed girl was showing the cake on a glass stand to anyone who could see over the people in front of them.

There was a push and a press as people, their mouths already watering, ogled the sticky delight.

'Congratulations!' said the girl to Lady Clanville-Smythe, handing her the cake stand, a bigger bouquet and a blue rosette with *2nd prize* embossed in gold letters in the middle. How the girl could hold so many things at once was a mystery, and shaking hands was quite a complicated manoeuvre but, once achieved, they both stood back, flustered but relieved, for the final award to be presented.

'In first place... a unanimous decision from our illustrious judges...' An even bigger trumpet flourish followed by a drum roll could be heard over the tannoy. The Fayre committee really were going overboard on the theatrics this year; but the crowd was absolutely loving it.

'This year's Perrimead-on-the-Wold County Cake Champion is...' The crowd teetered forward again, hyped up by sugar and drama in more or less equal quantities, to discover the name of the winner as the trumpet blast was broadcast yet again.

'A first, in every way for us all...' (my, how they loved that trumpet fanfare today) '...Lord Clanville-Smythe and his brilliant Battenburg cake!'

Lady Clanville-Smythe gasped. The crowd gasped, and then went berserk in rapturous applause while she remained astonished and with her mouth open – not a very lady-like posture to be sure. Could it be true? As far as she knew, her husband had never made anything more demanding than a piece of toast, and he'd even burnt that. Besides, he'd been at the barber's or in his room for almost two days; hadn't he?

Yet another almost identical girl appeared, carrying a vast, elaborate, gilded cake stand bearing what could easily be seen as a most exquisite cake. Significantly larger than the traditional Battenburg, this one had eight rows and eight columns of perfectly aligned pink and yellow squares. Every angle was an exact 90°, and the whole splendiferous delight was enrobed in a sugared marzipan cloak of cowslip yellow. Without doubt, it was a worthy winner.

The crowd continued to cheer and clap all over

again as the man who had pushed past the Viscountess earlier stepped up to receive his prize: the most enormous bouquet yet, a red rosette and a large engraved silver cup.

'Gerald!' she breathed admiringly, staring still open-mouthed at the clean-shaven man in front of her.

'I don't understand. I didn't recognise you. How did you…?'

Lord Clanville-Smythe, the beard and moustache-free 7th Viscount of Perrimead-on-the-Wold, winked at his wife. 'Chin up, Fenella. Thought I'd surprise you!' Leaning closer than he had been able to do for many months, he whispered, 'Ventured into the kitchen last night for a bit of thinking – fascinating place. Found an old cookbook with a stunningly good Battenburg recipe – think it was your grandmother's. Just increased the quantities a bit.'

Lady Clanville-Smythe smiled at her happy

husband who was acknowledging the crowd with a wave of the cup. She hadn't seen this much of his face in years and suddenly realised that underneath all that hair he was still a ruggedly handsome man.

'Oh Gerald, won't you miss it terribly?'

A pained look crossed her husband's face for a brief moment and fell off the other side with a thud.

'No, my dear,' he announced resolutely. 'I've decided not to. I think it's time for a new hobby and I've finally realised that, after all, *you* are what I've been missing.' And with that, he kissed her heartily – something that he also hadn't been able to do for many months.

The crowd loved it; they hadn't expected this kind of show. Truth to tell, Lady Clanville-Smythe was enjoying it too!

Lord Clanville-Smythe, 7th Viscount of Perrimead-on-the-Wold and home-made cake

County Champion gave a last victory wave to them all.

'I've spent so long with my grooming I almost forgot that I married you not my moustache,' he admitted ruefully. He looked her full in the face before continuing. 'I'm so sorry. You made me remember that when you chopped it off, Fenella. Thank you. Really; truly.' He cleared his throat noisily and wiped something from his cheek with his sleeve – his hands still being full of his Championship prizes.

'Now, let's go home for tea shall we?'

'Let's,' she smiled back, assured of his forgiveness, blushing like a schoolgirl and grasping the best cakes in the whole county.

Tea's The Thing!

Tea's The Thing!

There was a hustle and a bustle in the Royal kitchens. 6am and there were already jobs to be done: fireplaces to sweep, milk to collect from the front step, newspapers to iron, the cat to feed. Rosie and Lily, the Royal maids, were already occupied with these tasks which all needed to be done before breakfast. But, more important than all of these was the preparation of the Royal Tray.

First thing in the morning, the Queen liked to have a cup of tea in bed. She would sit up blearily, blow her nose on an enormous handkerchief from beneath her pillow, wipe the sleep from her eyes and, while a maid swished open the heavy curtains of her Monarchical boudoir, the Queen would sip tea from her special bone china cup, set on its matching saucer, while she contemplated the day ahead. The tea had to be hot, strong, unsweetened and with just the right amount of milk.

Everybody knew this and woe betide anyone who got it wrong. It was a habit she had begun as a girl; her father had done it before her and her grandmother before that. The Royal photo albums featured former Kings and Queens in sunshine and rain, all drinking tea on sandy beaches, on blustery moors, on stormy castle ramparts and on expensive yachts. Tea was the thing; always.

This morning, things were not going well. Jeffries, the butler, collected the teapot along with the china cup and saucer, ready for the morning brew to be made by the kitchen staff. He placed a snowy-white linen cloth on a silver tray and fetched the morning milk from the fridge, where Rosie had placed it not five minutes before. He had been butler for enough years to recognise when something was not quite right below stairs and, try as he might, he couldn't shake off that feeling this morning.

Nevertheless, he watched Lily sloosh water from the copper kettle round the pot to warm it as she did every morning, then empty it again before adding a spoonful from a canister bearing the Royal cipher, lifting the heavy kettle once more and filling the pot.

All as usual there he thought with understated pride. He walked six times round the hallway under the eagle eye of ancient royal portraits – the exact time required for the perfect brew to brew – and returned to oversee the carrying of the tray upstairs.

Cook was rolling pastry and wiping flour from her hair; the kitchen boy was running between the scullery and the stove, carrying dirty pans; the postman was putting the letters and bills through the flap in the back door; the cat was stretching lazily, having just jumped in through the open window. Yes, perhaps everything was as normal after all.

Or was it? Cook wouldn't look him in the eye and disappeared to fetch ingredients he could see already on the table; the kitchen boy ran out saying he 'just had to fetch something'; the maids were whispering together but stopped and shuffled nervously when he came in. Only the cat gazed unblinkingly at him. It was very curious.

Jeffries had no time to spare thinking about the strange morning, but he shifted the things slightly on the tray, tweaking the arrangement to his satisfaction as a skilled butler should. Every detail must be perfect for the Queen.

Just then, the clock on the mantlepiece struck 6.30am and the butler called Rosie to take the tea. But today, for some reason, Rosie was not eager to carry the tray. She didn't want to disobey her superior but was clearly uncomfortable.

'Is there a problem, Rosie?'

'Sorry Sir; I have a sore finger this morning. I seem to have trapped it in a door somehow. Might it be possible for Lily to take the tea today please?'

Jeffries raised his eyebrows and cleared his throat as he came to terms with the fact that this was not a smooth-running day after all.

'Very well. Lily? If you please…'

Lily was not pleased. In fact, she looked rather cross as she gave Rosie a hard nudge with her elbow and pursed her lips.

'Sorry Sir; I tripped over the cat yesterday and twisted my knee. I just don't think I can manage the stairs today.'

The Butler's eyebrows rose so high that they disappeared up under his hair and he cleared his throat several more times.

'Well, this is most irregular. Apparently *I* must take the Queen's tea, though it is not how we usually do things here. It is most unseemly for me to enter the bedroom of Her Majesty. Only her husband is allowed that privilege. Maids have been carrying the Queen her morning tea every day for over 50 years.'

The maids examined their shoes with feigned interest, but said nothing. Cook hovered in the doorway and the cat yawned rudely.

Picking up the tray with an ill-disguised sigh, the long-suffering butler made his way to the stairs and proceeded to navigate his way up towards the royal bedroom.

By the time he reached the top flight there had been a few wobbles – he was after all very out of practice – but not one drop had been spilt. Congratulating himself on his professionalism and pausing for breath after the exertion, Jeffries proceeded down the plush red carpet to the Queen's door, where he knocked twice and entered.

Her Majesty stirred as he placed the tray on an ornate table and did the curtain swishing that was usually Rosie's responsibility. Sunlight streamed in pleasingly, and by the time he'd turned around the Queen had blown her nose and was sitting up against plump pillows in readiness for her tea. She expressed surprise at seeing her trusty butler but royalty are, for the most part, used to taking things in their stride.

'Good morning, your Majesty.'

'Good morning, Jeffries. Everything all right?' she enquired.

'Absolutely, Ma'am.'

He thought it best not to embark on any explanation, but moved smoothly to the tray to pour the much-anticipated beverage which should now be the perfect temperature. The special cup was poured – there was something slightly odd about it but he couldn't identify it at that moment – and he handed it carefully to the Sovereign who puckered her nose in a most un-royal manner. Jeffries pretended not to notice and began to withdraw to allow her to drink her tea in peace.

He was stopped in his tracks by an indelicate spluttering from the four-poster bed and turned to see the Queen in a state of great agitation and distress with a spray of tell-tale drink all over the previously pristine sheet.

'What is the meaning of this?' demanded her majesty.

'Ma'am?'

'Jeffries, you and I have known one another for a considerable number of years and I ask you again, what is the meaning of this?' She lifted the cup in his direction indicating her displeasure.

'I'm sorry Ma'am, I don't understand.'

'This is not what I am used to. This is not how my morning begins. In fact, I don't believe this is even tea!'

'What?' exclaimed the butler and then, very

quickly to cover his involuntary reaction, 'I mean: I beg your pardon, Your Majesty. What seems to be the problem?'

'Taste it yourself,' commanded the Queen.

'Majesty?'

'Yes, Jeffries; I said, taste it yourself.'

It seemed an odd request but one does not disobey a royal command even in these modern times. Approaching the cup suspiciously, as if it were about to bite him on the nose, the butler first smelt the liquid and then put it to his lips.

'What do you think it is?' asked the Queen.

'Why Ma'am; I am sorry to say that I believe this might be… coffee.'

'Coffee?!!' the Queen spat out the words in much the same way that she had spat out the mouthful she had taken not a minute earlier. 'Why have you brought me coffee? I have tea in the mornings. You know that; everybody knows that. What in the world is going on that I have been brought coffee? It should be tea! Tea's the thing!'

So saying, her Majesty threw back the covers, crashed the cup back onto the saucer and marched from the room into the royal bathroom to begin her morning ablutions. She was not happy.

Neither was Jeffries, who scooped up the tray with stammering apologies and a face like thunder, that did not bode well for anyone below stairs. Fuming with shame, he set off to return to the kitchens.

'Coffee!' he announced plonking the tray next to the sink with such force that the cat shot out of the window in alarm. 'Tell me, who is responsible for this disaster?'

Nobody answered. In the silence a particularly large fly could be heard buzzing around Cook's head. She flapped at it with a floury hand.

'I said, who is responsible for this disaster?' Jeffries repeated his question in a voice that made the jam jars rattle.

Cook, now working on bread dough, punched it roughly. 'Nowt to do with me,' she puffed between phrases with the effort of kneading. 'The Cook… is not responsible… for the tea situation.' She nodded towards Lily and Rosie, 'That's their department.' And with that, she picked up a fearsome looking knife and began to score the top of the dough energetically.

'Ladies?' The butler's tone was one of exaggerated patience belying his increasing anger. 'Perhaps you would care to explain why I have been humiliated in front of my Queen this morning, to say nothing of her own inconvenience and her exposure to morning tea which failed most abominably to actually be drinkable. What is going on?'

Rosie shuffled her feet and twisted the corner of her apron in her fidgeting fingers while Lily, with a red face and trembling voice, owned up.

'I'm so sorry, sir,' her bottom lip trembled as

tears pricked her eyes. 'There was no tea in the canister this morning. I didn't know what to do, so I used coffee. I thought it might make a nice change…' Her voice trailed off.

'A nice change? A nice change?!' The butler snorted in disgust, 'If there's one thing you should have learnt by now it's that Her Majesty does not enjoy 'a nice change', or indeed, any change. Things are as they are because she likes them that way. This is outrageous! I have never been so embarrassed in my life.'

'Truly, sir,' Rosie chipped in, standing up for her friend, 'It wasn't really Lily's fault. There should have been more tea ordered last week. I don't know what the Housekeeper was thinking.'

Realising that the real responsibility for this disaster might lie elsewhere, the butler hurried out of the kitchen and headed to the Housekeeper's study where he planned to vent the full force of his own displeasure. After a perfunctory knock, he walked in to find the occupant at his desk, elbow deep in papers, a light sweat on his nose, his glasses balanced on his forehead, frowning at a computer screen and scratching his head all at once. This was Mr Harding, and he barely looked up.

'Hrrmpho,' he gave this unintelligible greeting because he also had a pencil clamped between his teeth.

'Harding,' Jeffries acknowledged the uncouth welcome with a nod, but getting scant other attention he was forced to rap on the desk with two fingers.

'Harding, I need to speak to you quite urgently.'

'Sorry, old chap,' the housekeeper replied, temporarily removing the pencil, readjusting his glasses and peering over them. 'Bit of bother with the new system. How can I help?'

'Apparently we are out of tea.'

'Tea?' came the vague reply as the harassed gentleman shuffled some papers, pushed his glasses up on top of his head again and tried to focus on his uninvited visitor.

'Indeed; The Queen was served coffee this morning instead.'

'Ooh, that's nice,' replied Mr Harding distractedly; he was a keen coffee drinker himself.

'No,' Jeffries corrected him, 'it was not nice; not nice at all. It was not nice for her and it most definitely was not nice for me. Moreover, I shall see to it that it is not nice for whoever is responsible. There should ALWAYS be tea available for Her Majesty at any time of day and night and I understand that you' – here he shook the same two fingers in the reddening face of Mr Harding – 'should have ordered more last week.'

Mr Harding looked most discomforted; he wriggled on his chair, furrowed his brow and shooed the cat off his desk who had just come through his office window hoping to escape the stress of the kitchen but not wanting to stay outside where it was starting to rain. The Housekeeper put the palms of his rather sweaty hands up in surrender.

'Look Jeffries, you may be right, but the truth is that I was on holiday in Broadstairs with my aunt last week and everything was in order when I left. I fail to see what else I could do. The fact is that more people are drinking coffee these days anyway so it's hardly a national crisis.'

The butler looked aghast at this dismissive turn of events and opened his mouth to protest violently. National crisis was exactly what it was.

He closed his mouth again as the harassed housekeeper stood and continued, 'I think you had better see the Master of the Household if you want to get to the bottom of this, but please do send my compliments to the Queen and let her know that coffee is considered a very fashionable drink in exalted circles these days. I believe the bishops and the House of Lords both drink it in vast quantities.'

And with that, Mr Harding sat down, returned his glasses to their functioning position on his nose, took a deep breath and turned his attention back to the puzzling screen.

Before Jeffries had time to pursue his line of enquiry with the Master of the Household, he was handed a note by an under butler summoning him to the Queen's office.

Her Majesty's habit was to shower, dress and spend an hour there before taking breakfast, perusing the newspaper headlines and checking the timetable for the day. She was always extremely busy and extremely efficient in her tasks and was loathe to waste a moment. Her butler trembled at the prospect of further questioning on the tea situation but, swallowing his pride and a large glass of water – his throat had become quite dry and tight at the prospect of this unscheduled meeting – he straightened his jacket and made his way to the office wing.

'Come!' said the familiar regal voice after he had knocked. Jeffries took yet another deep breath and obeyed.

Her Majesty had just got to a particularly interesting story about a man in Pucklechurch who believed he had found a cure for the common cold using artichokes, and wanted to finish her paragraph, so she ignored him for a full two minutes. This made the poor butler even more nervous and he fidgeted terribly, shifting his weight from one leg to the other.

'Extraordinary!' she pronounced when she'd finished and finally turned her attention to him. 'Well, Jeffries, I need hardly say how disappointed I am with the way this day has started.'

'Majesty... Ma'am,' he stuttered in reply. 'Once again I apologise... coffee... thought very fashionable in some quarters I am told... '

The Queen waved her hand at him dismissively

as if she were swatting at a particularly irritating fly.

'Nonsense Jeffries! Fashionable is hardly something that we are concerned about at the palace! Here we concern ourselves with important international events and matters of national importance. These, as you well know, require access to excellent tea at all times. Things are particularly busy at present and I believe I am receiving a delegation from Africa and India this afternoon, which may prove rather delicate. I cannot understand how this' – here Her Majesty paused, visibly shuddered, and willed herself to say the word '…coffee… situation came about, but I want it rectified immediately. Do you understand me? Resolved, sorted, corrected, remedied. Have I made myself clear?'

'Crystal, Ma'am,' came the subdued response.

'I'm so glad. That is all.'

And with that she turned her attention to the

horse racing section of the paper while Jeffries shuffled out disconsolately.

The Master of the Household was somewhat surprised to receive a visit from the butler that morning, but less surprised to hear the tale of the Royal tea since he had already heard it from several other members of staff including three cleaners and a man who'd come to look at the boiler. The news had made him rather uneasy. Evidently the butler was trying to pin the blame on someone and he was in no mood to be the scapegoat for the whole affair himself. Neither did he fancy being hauled over the coals by his Sovereign on the topic, and consequently poor Jeffries was given rather short shrift and told to be about his business.

Considering it wasn't even time for elevenses, the day really was going rather poorly for him so far. Jeffries pottered off to count the teaspoons again and hoped to goodness it would all be sorted out before 3.30pm when tea would be required all over again and probably earlier if there were to be visitors.

What he did not know was that the Master of the Household had indeed been in charge of ordering a number of necessities while the Housekeeper had been away on holiday with his aunt in Kent. He also did not know how tricky the new ordering system on the computer was; Mr Harding was wrestling with it even now, but the MotH (as we shall call him), had not really given his briefing enough attention in the meeting two weeks earlier. Since he was a whizz at some computer games he had been practising, he fancied himself as a bit of an IT expert but found himself all at sea when he logged in to make the necessary order from Mr Harding's office. Consequently, he had made rather a hash of it (the whole palace would have been running out of toilet roll as well had he not prudently bought in a box of twenty-four from home to try and cover his mistake).

The entire operation had been exacerbated by the cat who had jumped on his lap looking for affection and had then relaxed in a purring heap with his paw perilously near the computer keys. The inevitable had happened; the tea order had been deleted by a stretching paw just as he himself had pressed the 'send' button and, consequently, he had been blissfully unaware of the error.

Now you would think that all this could have been solved quite easily. Surely, after all someone could pop out to the shop and simply buy a packet of tea and be done with it? If the MotH could bring in toilet roll without discovery then amongst the entire palace staff someone, you may be saying, must have a spare box of tea at home? But, you would be mistaken.

You see her Majesty does not drink any old tea but a particular blend of different varieties of tea leaves plucked from the mountains of far away countries. This tea is, by tradition, made only for her and her household and the box bears a Royal coat of arms declaring her personal approval for the product. It is the envy of many other tea producers who have tried over the years to gain access to the Royal teapot and lure Her Majesty into drinking alternative tea made by a competitor. Nobody, until that morning, had been foolish enough to offer her coffee as a substitute.

Her Majesty had far too much to think about to refer to the tea situation at breakfast or indeed, all morning. She made do with orange juice with her toast and marmalade and cancelled elevenses completely as she was up to her ears in papers which needed to be signed; reports on milk production; projects to revive mining towns, and a speech which she needed to write for the state banquet next month, all of which would be discussed with the Prime Minister in their weekly meeting on Wednesday.

There was also the afternoon meeting with the Ambassadors of East Africa and Southern India which would be far from easy. The two countries had some issues with each other and as members of the Commonwealth family, Her Majesty had agreed, under pressure from the Foreign Office, to meet them both.

Since the Monarch has never been allowed to be anything but neutral in politics (in public anyway), she was not at all sure what was required of her. Perhaps she could sooth the tensions by showing them some famous paintings in her collection in the Royal Gallery or distract them with the latest news from the world of thoroughbred horse racing. Would that be of interest to them, she wondered? No matter, someone would bring her a folder shortly, full of relevant information and she would refresh her memory on what it was they were actually arguing about.

The Queen secretly believed that most disagreements could be sorted out quite amicable over a nice cup of tea, but that thought brought her right back to the unfortunate start to the day. The idea that one could reach the same level of friendship over coffee was quite ridiculous, she thought. Only tea could truly be relied upon for that.

The clock ticked on inevitably and all was quiet on the upper corridors. Below stairs however, things had been quite manic all morning with the MotH and Jeffries in particular trying to chase up delivery of the approved tea, post-haste. The tea company's website had crashed and Mr Harding could do nothing to fix that. In desperation the kitchen boy had been sent to the company's head office on the gardener's bike to procure some directly. Alas, a notice on the door informed him that they were closed for refurbishing for the next fortnight and the poor boy trembled as he pedalled back to deliver the bad news.

There was much throwing up of hands in despair, turning out of cupboards, drawers, shelves and even pockets in a vain attempt to find out whether a packet of Royal tea might have found its way to a dark corner, or been left forgotten at the back of somewhere.

Between them, the staff found a tin of peaches from 1972, three marbles, two socks – though not a pair (always the way, wherever you live) – twelve packets of Christmas shortbread, a postcard from Jeffries' holiday in Wales two years ago and an old five pence piece; but no tea.

Lunchtime came and went, served with sparkling or still water and a blend of juices, but no tea. The MotH was bold enough to ask her Majesty as she polished off her chocolate blancmange – a personal favourite of hers – whether coffee served perhaps with almond, oat, soy or even coconut milk might be more to her taste, but was treated to a look of such withering scorn that he seemed to visibly shrink and immediately regretted bringing it up.

'There's only one thing for it,' he announced to the exhausted staff back in the kitchen, 'we must make the blend ourselves.'

Everyone looked at him in horror. How could it be done?

'But, sir,' Jeffries protested, 'we simply don't have access to the speciality teas required.'

'I don't care!' The MotH was quite insistent. 'The Queen needs tea and tea she shall have. A delegation must go to the local stores and purchase a pack of every possible variety and we will combine the best right here in the kitchen.'

It was not a brilliant plan but it was the only one they had so, once again, the kitchen boy was sent in one direction, Lily and Rosie in another and Jeffries in a third. They had a single hour to gather the widest selection of teas possible. Meanwhile, the MotH was observed by Mr Harding, who wandered into the kitchen to make himself a coffee a short while later, to be laying a cloth across the old table onto which he placed every saucepan, jug and pot he could lay his hands on and, in the middle of it all, an ancient set of weighing scales. Clearly something big was afoot, but Mr Harding was too embroiled in trying to detangle the on-line ordering system to invite any more drama into his day, so slipped out again after taking two chocolate biscuits from the tin. (Normally he was only allowed one, but since Cook wasn't there to complain, he thought he'd chance it; after all, he needed to get his strength up for this infernal computing lark.)

At 2.22pm the Ambassadors of both India and Kenya were escorted from the front door, up the sweeping staircase and along a series of corridors where every step of their overly polished shoes was muffled by opulent, thick carpet.

Jeffries, somewhat hot, bothered and dishevelled having visited a coffee house on the off chance they might also have some tea he could purchase, and from where he was ejected with some force but without apology, had literally run back to perform his afternoon duties and recognised that the stress of the day was starting to get to him.

He showed the honourable gentlemen to leather seats outside the Queen's reception room and waited in silence trying not to show how out of breath he still was. The two smartly dressed men neither spoke nor looked at each other. They sat very stiffly, their hands clasped around unidentifiable boxes and tried to pretend they were invited to palaces pretty much every day. They were not, and Jeffries was not taken in for a moment. Their nerves were evident in the way one gripped his mysterious box so tightly that his knuckles were completely white; the other repeatedly rubbed each of his shoes against the back of his opposite trouser leg in an attempt to increase their shine.

Somewhere a grandfather clocked chimed the half hour and Jeffries stepped forward, knocked and entered. He turned sharp right, bowed to an unseen figure and announced the two gentlemen who, after trying to banish their awkwardness, rose and followed him in.

The Queen was standing next to a walnut table on which stood a lamp, a photograph of a winning race horse, complete with rosette, and a small bell by which she would summon Jeffries when the meeting was over.

'Thank you,' she nodded to her butler. 'You may bring tea in fifteen minutes.'

Then, turning to her visitors she offered her hand to be shaken before taking a seat and inviting them to sit down as well.

Jeffries bowed and exited as calmly as he could. Once out of the room, he sprinted back along the corridor and slid down the bannisters at alarming speed – a thing he hadn't contemplated for over twenty years – saving every spare second in order to see how the tea blending experiment was going in the kitchen.

Not well, was the obvious answer.

Strewn across the table lay multiple boxes of every tea you could imagine and some you will never have imagined unless you were to have a very serious fever. There were liquorice teas, fruit teas, herb teas, spiced teas, something that looked like flower petals, something else that looked like the contents of a hamster cage that has just been cleaned out (not pleasant), brand named boxes, own brand boxes, loose leaf teas and tea bags – the square, round and pyramid varieties. The smell was just extraordinary and the noise was increasing as every member of staff tried to create their own blend, leaning and stretching, stirring and mashing, adding and measuring complex combinations to the mugs in front of them. The kettle was screeching as it boiled and multiple pans of boiling water bubbled on the stove as the MotH struggled to keep up the supply to pour onto each unique concoction before it could be tasted and tested.

An argument had broken out between Lily and Rosie over who had taken all the camomile tea while Cook had turned an interesting shade of green after discovering that a combination of rhubarb and ylang-ylang really did not agree with her at all.

The MotH was madly trying to write down every one's recipes in the right proportions – 'Yes, but did you use a pinch or a smidgen? Be precise or we'll never be able to make it again.' 'Was that a teaspoon or a tablespoon that you used?' 'Did you say rose-hip or rose petal?'

Discarded cups and mugs covered every inch of table that wasn't otherwise covered in ingredients.

Spills and stains of every hue crept across the cloth; one variety of tea was getting muddled with another. Clearly, no one had yet managed to come up with a tea remotely like the one the Queen was going to require in less than a quarter of an hour. It was pandemonium.

Jeffries didn't know whether he was about to faint or explode; the pressure was unbearable.

'People!' he gasped weakly, clapping his hands together for emphasis and to be heard. 'People; we have approximately ten minutes to complete this task. The Queen has ordered tea for herself and her visitors and we must deliver it, come what may.'

The blood drained from every face at the table as the reality of the situation sunk in. The prospect of failing their Monarch hit each one with the force of an express train; it was not to be contemplated. Failure was not an option.

With renewed vigour, the staff got back to work, shouting, straining and sipping their teas while

Jeffries slowly prepared a fresh tray to take back upstairs.

Things upstairs weren't going terribly well either. The honourable ambassadors were showing themselves to be rather dishonourable as their replies to the Queen's enquiries were filled with slights and subtle insults to one another. The Royals, as I'm sure you know, are highly regarded for their tact and diplomacy, but even a Sovereign must have her limitations.

The Queen had understood that the argument between the two nations represented in front of her was something to do with their national exports, the major one of which was – quite coincidentally – tea.

The situation appeared to be that each one was trying to undermine the other in sending their best leaves to Europe where tea drinkers were on the increase and therefore where maximum profits could be made. Upon this depended the welfare of their people, and consequently the prosperity of their respective nations. The irony was not lost on the Queen, who was herself anticipating a cup of her favourite beverage any moment now. Surely whatever disaster had been unleashed downstairs this morning must be sorted out by now. The ambassadors were getting more and more worked up, redder and redder in the face, and a tea interruption would be very welcome.

It was with some relief that her Majesty responded to Jeffries knock and he entered with a truly magnificent tray. An antique, silver tea pot towered over a matching milk jug and sugar bowl which nestled next to three exquisite fine china cups and saucers each accompanied by a recently polished antique tea spoon.

'Ma'am,' he announced, having placed it all on a low sideboard and taken his place to one side, poised to pour.

'Lovely; thank you.' The Queen threw him a

grateful glance while taking in his somewhat flustered appearance before turning to her guests. 'Gentlemen, perhaps we could take this opportunity to drink some tea together? Tea's the thing after all.'

The ambassadors looked as though they'd like to throw each other something far more damaging, than a glance, but nodded politely.

The African gentleman, suddenly remembering something, picked up his box and advanced to the tea tray.

'Your Majesty, excuse me; I should have presented this earlier. It is a present from the highlands of my country, a famous tea growing area. I hope you will enjoy this gift.'

'How lovely,' murmured the Queen and stepped forward to take the present.

'But, your Majestic Majesty,' interrupted the Indian ambassador, tripping over his words in his eagerness and kicking himself that he hadn't presented his own gift first. 'Madam, I also have an offering from our own even more famous hillsides, donated by the esteemed national tea growers guild and sent with their extreme compliments and blessing.'

The Queen took a pace backwards to allow space for the Asian man who had (quite rudely) stepped between them.

A most indecorous scuffle ensued as the two men tried to step in front of each other to ensure that the Queen accepted their own tea first. This rapidly descended into pushing and shoving as inevitably, hair was pulled, noses were pinched and elbows found tummies. Both Jeffries and The Queen were horrified and the Monarch took temporary refuge behind a leather chair.

'I offered mine first,' growled the African.

'But mine is better,' insisted the Indian.

Her Majesty rolled her eyes at their childish display and was just about to intervene when both men, their boxes of tea now opened to display the quality of their superior product to the other, tripped over an Axminster rug and sent the contents in an impressive arc across the room where the tea leaves pattered like spring rain on the tray cloth.

'Well,' breathed her Majesty as if she had just caught two naughty boys up to mischief. 'I hope you're proud of yourselves. Look at my carpet!'

It was true, there was a trail of brown leaves sprinkled amongst the design of the rug but the majority lay in a heap on the tray.

'Perhaps you will allow me, Ma'am?' enquired Jeffries smoothly stepping in.

The Queen nodded in a mixture of relief and infuriation, and sat down. A reviving cup of tea was exactly what she needed right now. Tea, once again, would be the thing.

With his back to the room, the Queen's butler busied himself with the tray and subsequently presented first Her Majesty and then the ambassadors with a steaming cup of hot tea before taking up his place again.

The Queen blew across the top of her cup before taking a sip. She frowned, swallowed and pondered.

'New blend, Jeffries?'

'Er… yes, your Majesty. In honour of the occasion, it was felt appropriate…'

'Extraordinary.'

She took another sip, then another, and then a most un-royal gulp as she relaxed back into the chair temporarily forgetting her unruly visitors.

The ambassadors drank and appreciative noises were made as they too felt the flavoursome tea go to work on their anxieties and cares. Closing their eyes, each tea drinker floated away in their imagination to somewhere green, warm and with a restorative pleasant breeze which revived both their minds and their bodies. They were roused by a small cough from the butler.

'More tea, Majesty?'

'Absolutely,' Her Royal Highness affirmed, nodding contentedly.

'Gentlemen?' Jeffries attended to the guests who were equally enthusiastic.

'So do tell us all, Jeffries. These gentlemen are, apparently, tea enthusiasts themselves so will appreciate the detail. It is quite remarkable tea, but what is it?'

Jeffries took a deep breath and wondered how honest he should be. In truth he had brought upstairs nothing but a teapot full of hot water, leaving downstairs the ruined debris of the multiple tea blending experiments, each of which had ended in abject failure, and a number of devastated staff members.

The accidental arrival on his tray of two individually exquisite varietals of tea was entirely good luck. That he had been able to spoon the mixture up and into the pot unnoticed was greater luck, but the best luck of all was blending a combination of the two which had been greeted with rapture by everyone, but most importantly by her Majesty.

'Well,' sighed the Queen decisively, 'I think we all know what this means. Your problem has been solved gentlemen. From now on both of your great countries will supply tea to the palace where my newly appointed tea-blender' – here she looked at Jeffries – 'will oversee its production into an innovative fusion of afternoon delight which will receive my personal seal of approval and be marketed to the entire country bearing my coveted Royal Coat of Arms. It's too good to keep it to myself and it's only right that Jeffries' involvement be recognised. Tea is always, most definitely, the thing gentlemen! We shall call it *The Jeffries Gem Afternoon Blend.*'

And so it was that international diplomacy was

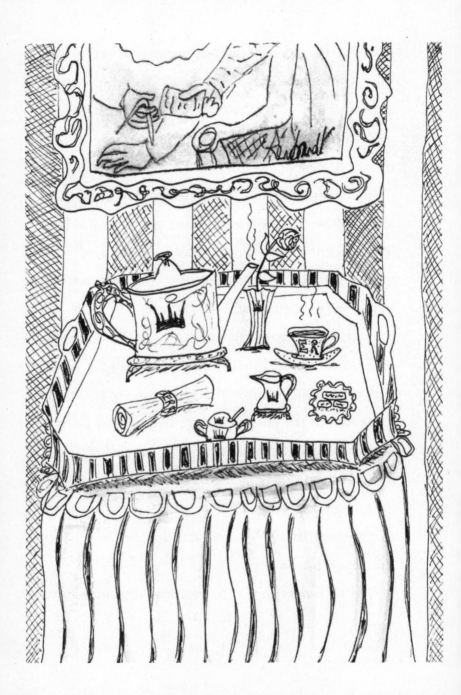

restored; two abashed but very happy ambassadors shook hands with one another with smiles and apologies, bowed formally to the Head of the Commonwealth and returned to their respective embassies with good news for tea growers in both East Africa and southern India.

Jeffries laid aside his gloves and uniform for his promotion to Royal tea-blender; the under-butler filled the Butler's position very capably, while a footman took on his role; two nations were friends once more and, best of all, her Majesty was never offered coffee again.

Below stairs the evidence of the afternoons catastrophic attempts at tea blending was thankfully bundled up and thrown away, along with the rogue canister of coffee, so that life could go back to normal for everyone; which it did.

Except for the cat who had helped herself to the remnants of the beverage blending debacle and was sick for a week.

What's In A Name?

What's In A Name?

Algernon Montgomery Lysander Ignatius Quentin Horatio Harold Ambrose Fitzwilliam Grantley-Ponsonby was not a learnèd man. He did terribly poorly at school. With such a long name to contend with, it took him all lesson just to write it at the top of each sheet of paper. Even then, he had to use teeny tiny letters to fit it all in, so it always ended up very squashed and barely legible. More often than not, when it came to exams, everyone else had finished by the time he had simply written his name. There had even been occasions when the examiner couldn't make out what he had written, and then he had been known to lose marks before ever gaining any. It was not a happy time.

Things did not get easier when he left school. By the time he had filled in any job applications, the position had been taken by someone with a nice short name like John, Jack or Jane. University was out of the question since he had no fancy certificates at all, except his birth certificate bearing the fearfully long name: Algernon Montgomery Lysander Ignatius Quentin Horatio Harold Ambrose Fitzwilliam Grantley-Ponsonby, and which had required a special non-regulation, double-size document to fit everything on it.

'Why ever did we give him such an unmanageable name?' asked his father for the 30 millionth time. 'Look at all the trouble it has caused.'

Being a sweet-natured woman, his mother counted to ten, as she always did before replying to this particular question from her husband. Taking a deep breath and forcing a smile, she looked up from her book: 'Sweetness, surely you remember that it was your father's dying wish that our son carry on the family name.'

'Hrrrumph,' replied Mr Grantley-Posonby senior, scratching his neck uncomfortably, and wishing yet again that his father's name had been Nigel.

His parents did not want their son to lie in bed all day counting the damp patches on the ceiling, or making a nuisance of himself in the kitchen. Neither would they allow their ill-qualified boy to sit around the house watching daytime television, waste his time wandering round the garden, or gazing out of the window in a daydream.

Indeed, at that very moment, Algernon Montgomery Lysander Ignatius Quentin Horatio Harold Ambrose Fitzwilliam Grantley-Ponsonby was doodling on the steamed up window of the drawing room, apparently oblivious to the fact that he was the subject of his parent's discussion.

Something had to be done.

'He can't be a doctor,' fretted his frowning father, 'it takes years of study and requires enormous intelligence.' He began to pace around the room like a caged tiger; this was never a good sign. 'He can't be an astronaut for the same reason,' his disappointed father went on.

The volume of his voice increased with every profession he listed, while his wife went nervously back to her book. 'He can't be a nuclear physicist or a high court judge; he can't be a marine biologist or a chemical engineer. He can't be an archeologist or a teacher since he is a total dunderhead who has apparently learnt nothing! What else is there?'

He drummed his fingers on the top of the grand piano, muttered, and frowned. It didn't always help him think any better but it made him feel purposeful. On this occasion however, inspiration appeared to strike. 'I say, perhaps he could become a vicar; that's very respectable.'

But poor Algernon Montgomery Lysander Ignatius Quentin Horatio Harold Ambrose Fitzwilliam Grantley-Ponsonby could barely pronounce words like 'ecclesiology' and 'eschatology'. He didn't care for the robes, was overwhelmed by the vast quantities of theological reading material required, and the sound of church bells pealing, quite frankly, gave him the heebie-jeebies. He hated speaking in public since he was convinced everyone was laughing at his ludicrous name all the time and quite often, unfortunately, they were. He came sadly home where his father shook his head in exasperation and his mother made him some hot chocolate to cheer him up.

It seemed there would be no glittering career for their son; he simply didn't have the grandiose aspirations which his father in particular, had anticipated.

Instead, Algernon Montgomery Lysander Ignatius Quentin Horatio Harold Ambrose Fitzwilliam Grantley-Ponsonby was frequently to be found lying on the lawn, staring at the cloud pictures he could see forming in the sky, lurking in the old greenhouse and around the vegetable patch, or plunging his hands into the black soil as if he were digging for treasure.

'Very odd,' noted his father testily. 'Do you think we should take him to a doctor?'

'Honestly, darling,' replied his wife, 'I do think we should let him find his own way.'

'Nonsense!' Mr Grantley-Ponsonby senior was not inclined to modern notions of parenting. His fingers began to drum again.

'Ha!' he exclaimed suddenly, frightening Mrs Grantley-Ponsonby and causing her to drop her knitting, her book and the cat all at once. 'I have it!'

'Do you dear?' she responded weakly, her voice

muffled as she tried to retrieve everything from under the sofa. The cat was not co-operative. 'I'm so glad.'

'Of course! He will join the navy immediately. They take anyone I hear. It's the obvious solution.'

Mrs Grantley-Ponsonby opened her mouth to reply, but thought it prudent to close it again.

So, Algernon Montgomery Lysander Ignatius Quentin Horatio Harold Ambrose Fitzwilliam Grantley-Ponsonby was packed off to sea with a kiss from his mother and a hearty clap on the back from his father.

Surprisingly, he was not completely opposed to the idea, even though no one had actually asked him what he wanted to do.

He had always dreamed of growing things. He liked the way tiny seeds could bloom into the most extraordinary plants – or trees – of wonderfully dazzling colours, and marvellous shapes and sizes. That is why the garden at home had been one of his favourite places. It was a refuge of calmness and order, where nature flourished and brought him hours of pleasure regardless of his dreadful examination results.

The library was full of gardening books and they had appealed to him because he could look at the beautiful colour pictures without having to wrestle with the complicated science of it all. He discovered that many of the plants had strange Latin names written in small letters underneath; some of them were almost as long as his own which, for a few short moments, made that feel almost normal. On some very bleak days, he had come to think of these plants as his friends.

Out in the ocean, Algernon Montgomery Lysander Ignatius Quentin Horatio Harold Ambrose Fitzwilliam Grantley-Ponsonby, like all the other naval recruits, was called by his last name, and as everyone was always in a tremendous hurry to bark out orders and crack on with naval activities, he was simply known as 'Ponsonby'. People still nudged each other and sniggered at him behind his back and sometimes, if they were particularly rude, in front of him, but what with all the splicing of the mainsail, battening down the hatches, swabbing the decks, and learning his baggywinkle* from his ballast, there wasn't much time to spare for self-pity. Besides, he was used to it.

They sailed in a fine ship called *The Albertina*, which had weathered many storms but still ruled the waves of the seven seas with dignified magnificence. All the new recruits were put through their paces with a tough training regime. They learnt to sleep in hammocks, climb ropes, unfurl sails, tie complicated knots, understand basic navigation using the stars, and read the weather patterns and ocean currents.

The Captain was a kind man but he had no time

---

* *baggywinkle* – soft covering for ropes which prevents them chafing the sails

for shilly-shallying. He ruled the upper deck, strode meaningfully around the lower decks greeting the men by name, and puzzled over the maps in his cabin until he saw double. He expected immediate obedience from his crew and he got it. He quite literally ran, as they say, 'a tight-ship' and his sailors liked it that way.

All but Algernon Montgomery Lysander Ignatius Quentin Horatio Harold Ambrose Fitzwilliam Grantley-Ponsonby, who found that although he wasn't seasick and loved the fresh salty air on his face each day, he missed green, growing things with an ache he never knew a man could have.

They had been at sea for almost a year, through raging storms and hopeless calms; they saw whales and walruses, porpoises and pirates; they saw the northern lights and the Southern Cross but had no orders to land anywhere. Even the hardiest sea-faring man began to long for a good home-cooked meal and solid earth beneath his feet; they even began to wonder whether they were lost...

This was the state of things when, one long dark night, when supplies were almost as low as morale, a fierce north-easter blew up a storm that sent the ship into a spin. Waves as high as twenty-storey buildings tossed the vessel around as though it were a cork in a bucket. Even the Captain found himself turning a lurid shade of green, and everyone's lunch returned to the ocean in a violent and disgusting manner, as men stumbled to retch over the sides.

The ship pitched and twirled, hurling itself around so that everyone thought they must surely drown. Men lashed themselves to the mast, knelt below deck to say prayers and clutched photos of their loved ones to their rapidly beating hearts. Once again, everyone except Algernon Montgomery Lysander Ignatius Quentin Horatio Harold Ambrose Fitzwilliam Grantley-Ponsonby.

He was not for one moment troubled by the storm. Our hero may not have got to grips with his school books but he could swim like a fish. When a particularly large wave swept him off his feet and over the side, this talent proved enormously useful.

The coldness of the water was a terrific shock, and at first he was rather frightened but, after spitting out a mouthful of sea water, he struck out in a determined fashion. Miraculously, the strong current and crashing waves carried him safely away from the *Albertina*, but the freezing ocean began to suck the life out of him. His swimming strokes got slower and slower; strange spots of light began to dance in front of his eyes and before long he blacked out completely.

Amazingly, the ship survived the night. True, there were some gashes in the canvas sails and some barrels had been lost into the sea, but she was basically sound. In the calm of a new day, the

Captain took a register of his men and discovered that they were all accounted for, except one.

Ruefully, the crew held a special ceremony for their fellow sailor who, they all assumed, must have been washed overboard and drowned. They even made a memorial wreath using the special sailor's knots they had learnt and lowered it respectfully over the side, where it bobbed away peacefully towards the distant horizon.

Algernon Montgomery Lysander Ignatius Quentin Horatio Harold Ambrose Fitzwilliam Grantley-Ponsonby had not drowned. After many hours, floating unconscious in the ocean like a piece of driftwood, he was washed up on a distant and exotic island with sandy shores, and curious plants which grew as far as the eye could see.

There on the gritty, golden sand the warmth of the sun slowly revived him after his ordeal. Fortunately, in his unconscious state he had not encountered any sharks, neither had he been dashed to pieces on sharp rocks, nor had he been cut to ribbons on the coral reef of the island where the azure waves broke in rhythmic succession. All in all it was a remarkably lucky escape in every possible sense.

He could hardly believe his good fortune and, for the first time in a very long time, when he gained consciousness and realised he was both safe and completely alone, he smiled. He may have been shipwrecked and with no possible means of escape, but Algernon Montgomery Lysander Ignatius Quentin Horatio Harold Ambrose Fitzwilliam Grantley-Ponsonby was not remotely perturbed by that.

He set out almost immediately (once his legs felt less wobbly) to explore the island by, very sensibly, walking around the edge of the entire place to get a sense of its size. He knew better than to simply plough into the undergrowth of a place he had never been. There was no knowing how many hazards he might meet: wild animals, swamps, man-eating plants, vertical drops, rabid biting insects or the like.

No, our new castaway may not have been top of the exam charts but he was not by any means a stupid man. By circumnavigating the island he was also able to keep a look out for anything that might help him in this new life that had been thrust on him.

He made a mental note of freshwater streams that ran down to the shore and drank deeply from the first one he came to, thankful that he had made the discovery so soon. Fresh water is, after all, the first requirement for human survival.

He took note of secluded bays, rocky tidal pools where he might be able to catch some fish trapped by the retreating tide, and some higher ground in the middle of the island, as well as a series of interesting caves. There was no sign of human habitation but a quantity of fruit-bearing trees which could provide some nourishment grew on the sheltered slopes further inland. He picked a few and carefully broke them open and rubbed them on his skin, because he was well aware that some of the most appetising-looking plants can be poisonous to humans. Best to test for any unpleasant reactions on his skin first. He really was far more sensible than his parents had ever given him credit for.

It took several hours to get back to the point from which he had started and Algernon Montgomery Lysander Ignatius Quentin Horatio Harold Ambrose Fitzwilliam Grantley-Ponsonby had, also very sensibly, marked that point with a pile of stones which he had gathered from beneath the tree line before he began. By then, the sun was dipping into the ocean and the light was fading fast and he needed both food and shelter.

Because he was quite agile – all that swimming had helped his fitness – the former naval recruit shimmied up a tree and tied himself securely to a branch with his own leather belt so he wouldn't fall out during the night when he was asleep. His tummy was rumbling quite loudly, but he daren't risk eating the fruit he had gathered yet and there was no point searching for anything else until there was some daylight again.

The new day dawned clear and calm, as they always did in this secluded part of the world. Algernon Montgomery Lysander Ignatius Quentin Horatio Harold Ambrose Fitzwilliam Grantley-Ponsonby was none the worse for spending the night up a tree, apart from a little stiffness in his shoulders, but he did a few stretches on the sandy beach to prepare himself for some strenuous activity.

There were no lumps or bumps on his skin, no unsightly rash or ominous swelling, so he took the remains of the fruits he had experimented with the night before and ate them slowly for his breakfast.

Thus fortified, he embarked on the necessary projects of building a shelter.

He had a knack for picking the trees with bendy branches that he could weave together and lashed whole panels together using trailing vines which he plaited together to ensure they were strong enough to keep his new home upright. He revisited the stream of clear fresh water and discovered that he could hollow out other branches to fashion carrying utensils. Collecting drinking water was the next task and he gladly undertook it.

The days unfolded gloriously, one into another as he set about starting a new life away from orders, away from people and away from the burden of having to keep telling anyone his terrible name.

Every morning saw him exploring his new paradise, swimming in the bluest of blue seas, diving for lobsters and unusual shells which he used to decorate his new home. Hours were spent tasting juicy and flavoursome (previously unknown) fruits, taking cuttings, nurturing seedlings and experimenting with propagating, and even creating entirely new plants by grafting one fantastic plant onto another.

At last his dream of growing things was coming true and he loved every solitary moment of it. Life was idyllic. Each day was an adventure spent beneath towering vegetation; a place where flowers brightened each moment and strange shrubs flourished under his ministrations.

The island provided everything he needed. He even came across some wild goats, the offspring of domesticated animals left behind by smugglers who, years before, had also taken advantage of the caves he had discovered on the opposite side of the island.

Algernon Montgomery Lysander Ignatius Quentin Horatio Harold Ambrose Fitzwilliam

Grantley-Ponsonby watched and waited, seeing which plants the goats enjoyed the most and then, he cleverly coaxed them into a pen he had made so he could use their milk. He hated to see animals locked up and took to only putting them in the pen at night so they didn't wander off too far. Since he brought them their favourite plant fodder every day, the goats were happy with this arrangement and they settled down well together. He could have milk, butter, cheese and yoghurt and even meat if he wanted it, but he was just as happy with the fish, the crabs and the shellfish which he trapped in the rock pools.

He experimented with the bounty of the island and made a unique kind of bread from coconut flour (which he pounded using a smooth stone) mixed with goats milk, and then cooked on a rock in the midday sun while he napped in the shade of one of his giant plants.

Each night he lay down on a banana leaf bed

and looked at a canopy of stars peeping between the woven house, until he slept deeply and peacefully. He could not have wished for a better life. There were no exams; no one telling him he should be doing something else; no homework; no paperwork at all and definitely no-one asking him to tell them his name or write it down anywhere at all. He was thoroughly content with the company of so many acres of striking, colourful plants who cared not one whit for who their caretaker was.

It was like a heavenly dream. If that's what it was, he hoped he would never wake up.

So, his life would have continued in this far-flung bliss had it not been for the fastidious map makers of home who, many, many years later, were sent to make new maps for the navy in the hope that fewer ships would get lost on their voyages across the oceans.

The young man who had left for the navy was an old man by now; one who had almost forgotten

that dreadfully long name, and who was taken completely by surprise when, alerted by the mad bleating of his goats (who had flourished so much that they had produced several generations of offspring and now numbered over one hundred), he watched a crowd of explorers, cartographers, scientists and government officials turn up on his beach.

Our hero had been engrossed in fertilising his newest seedlings with an experimental concoction, and was horrified to find his private paradise had been invaded. Armed with clipboards, cameras, computers, and scientific paraphernalia, the strangers swarmed through his home and across the whole island like an army of ants.

They destroyed both the peace and his years of work, carelessly trampling his plants and endlessly measuring distances, angles and altitudes until he wanted to scream. His gardens were ruined beyond repair; all his labour and loving care lay squashed in the mud. It was hardly surprising then, that a solitary tear squeezed itself out of one eye and trickled slowly down his sunburnt cheek.

The castaway was devastated by the noise, the intrusion, the lack of care for nature's bounty and the sheer number of chattering human beings who jostled for his attention. And then there were the never-ending questions. Who was he? Why was he here? How long had he been here? How had he survived? He refused to answer any of them; he just shook his head sadly and walked slowly away.

He retreated to the sanctuary of the quiet caves on the other side of the island which the scientists didn't seem to care for. In truth, he could hardly remember the answers to any of those questions; he had almost forgotten how to talk to people at all. These past years had been spent with his accepting friends, the plants, and though he hummed a tune to them from time to time and occasionally broke out into a full-throated whistle, he had not used words for many a long day.

His memories were blurred. While he could recall the night of the storm during which he had been able to escape the naval life and begin an entirely new one, everything before that was fragmented, uncertain, like a thought that dissolves in morning mist. His parents would have been horrified, except of course they had been told that their son had tragically drowned. They mourned him, laid a memorial stone for him and had, inevitably, grown old and died themselves in the succeeding years.

The officials and experts scratched their heads and whispered together. They collected samples, wrote things down, logged in data, sketched diagrams and calculated formulae; they dug up plants, avoided the goats when they could (who also detested their arrival and were inclined to butt them with their sharp horns), and put the remnants of plants in jars.

It seemed they would never leave.

When the visitors finally ran out of things to collect – largely because they had ruined so many – they did not feel in good conscience that they could leave the castaway there. In many ways, they felt that he was their greatest discovery of all and some of them foresaw prizes and honorary degrees being showered upon their academic heads in recognition of such an amazing find. They became quite puffed up with pride at the thought of such glittering awards.

Clearly the strange, bearded man understood them, even though he still would not speak, and was less than eager to board their ships. He frequently wandered back to his devastated gardens, hoping against hope that the unwelcome visitors would have left and he could pick up the threads of his tranquil life again.

It was not to be.

Together, the research team decided it was their

absolute duty to bring the man back to England; back to civilisation. Besides, he obviously had a skill with plants and a vast knowledge of the exotic flora of this tropical island, from which the Royal Horticultural Society would benefit enormously.

They messaged home to say they had found an extraordinary and highly skilled plant specialist who had grown things of such splendour that it quite took your breath away. They even sent some pictures of how the plants had looked before their foolish feet had blundered through, and over, them all.

So, at last, the pack of explorers packed up their equipment and prepared to return home. Since their reluctant host resisted their efforts to get him aboard, I am sorry to say that they waited until he was asleep, and simply rolled him up in his banana leaf bed and carried him up the gangplank along with a few unusual pot plants they had rescued from the wreckage of their trip. By the time he woke up his island home was many miles behind him.

Our long-named hero felt betrayed. The sense of loss was overwhelming and he spent the voyage leaning over the stern, his eyes squinting and scanning the horizon, trying to discern some sign of his paradise, now lost. He paced the deck at night, bereft without the familiar island smells, unable to sleep without the relaxing lullaby of gently breaking waves on his very own beach. He mourned the loss of his life's work, eyeing the bell jars and test tubes of mangled leaves and roots with mounting sorrow. What would his life be now?

The nearer the ship came to England, the more agitated he became. Although he had forgotten most of his earlier life, he realised with sorrow that he would no longer be able to live on a golden shore, sleep on a banana-leaf bed or enjoy the freedom to wander at will through a jungle Eden. A throbbing pain began to grow in his stomach, an aching dread of something he couldn't quite put his finger on.

There was a ripple of excitement amongst the crew and the scientists when land was sighted at last. They called one another by name to come and look, and in that moment a memory stirred as all at once, Algernon Montgomery Lysander Ignatius Quentin Horatio Harold Ambrose Fitzwilliam Grantley-Ponsonby recognised the looming shadow he was carrying.

In all his years in that wonderful place of tranquility, he had never once heard his ridiculously long name spoken and neither had he needed to utter it himself. It came to him now like an inflatable rising from the depths of a pool, shifting and writhing, blurred and dim until it resolved itself into the monstrosity that he had almost forgotten. The freedom of escape he had enjoyed retreated skittishly and, instead, he felt a dull weight descending in his mind, beginning to crush him. And it almost succeeded.

The scientists and map makers received a thundering welcome back in London.

There were balloons and streamers, cheering crowds, flags and a marching band. As the ship docked, a throng of well-wishers and dignitaries swarmed to welcome the returnees.

Among them was the esteemed representative from the Royal Horticultural Society wearing the freshest, biggest yellow buttonhole that he could find in his own garden that morning. His name was Ernest Pennyweather and he was eager to meet the plant genius he knew was coming with the team. He had spent some considerable time that morning deciding what to wear for the important occasion. He wasn't at all sure what the correct form of dress was for meeting a plant genius and had opted in the end for a very unsuitable tweed suit complete with matching waistcoat and silk tie. The whole ensemble was scratchy and hot but he forgot all about that as he scanned the ship for the gentleman he was to receive.

When a thin, tanned old figure with a far away look in his faded blue eyes came slowly into view, clutching an unusual plant Ernest had never seen before, he knew he had found his man and longed to glean all the treasures of his new guest's plant knowledge as soon as possible.

A brass band burst into the national anthem and streamers were launched into the air. Forgetting his manners, pushing past the Mayor and straightening his tie, Ernest was the first to smile at the stranger and shake him enthusiastically by the hand as he stepped off the boat and onto the land he had left so many years ago.

'Welcome to England, sir!' Mr Pennyweather burbled, blushing to be in the presence of such an evident genius. 'Or should I say, 'Welcome Home'?' He gave a nervous laugh but squashed it as he noted that the returnee was not registering any amusement at his feeble joke. 'I,... er... we, are delighted to see you looking so well. I have been looking forward to meeting you so very, very much. The Royal Horticultural Society is very much, absolutely, at your service.'

Mr Pennyweather gave an exaggerated and completely unnecessary bow. There was an awkward pause; the stranger didn't seem to be quite as excited as the crowds who were still yelling and stomping on the quay. The RHS representative was regretting his choice of suit and was aware of a prickly itch working its way up his left leg. He tried to ignore it and instead mopped his brow with his handkerchief while looking expectantly at the newcomer.

'Ah, sir… Are you all right old chap? My name is Ernest Pennyweather – huge fan by the way. Perhaps … you might like … sorry, didn't see it in the notes I was sent… to tell me your name?'

There was another, longer pause. The stranger looked around him at the sights and sounds of a country he had all but forgotten, and he blinked in the pale sunlight. Nothing looked the same. He turned his head to take in the unfamiliar coast line, the modern buildings scrunched together and the still seething throng. The sound of cars, engines and people merged together in a blaring symphony that hurt his poor head.

Perhaps there was something familiar about this after all. He looked again into the eager eyes of Ernest Pennyweather and something blurry uncoiled and slowly came into focus in the memory of Algernon Montgomery Lysander Ignatius Quentin Horatio Harold Ambrose Fitzwilliam Grantley-Ponsonby. The weight he had felt on the ship vanished as a vibrant, exciting idea broke into his mind like the promise of the sunrise on a new day.

He looked at the crowds; he looked back at the sea and slowly he smiled to himself. He couldn't go back to his island – truth to tell, he wasn't even quite sure exactly where that was – but he didn't have to go back to whatever his life was before the island either.

He would go on, and he would go on, on his own terms.

Algernon Montgomery Lysander Ignatius Quentin Horatio Harold Ambrose Fitzwilliam Grantley-Ponsonby refused to be bullied by his name anymore.

Taking a firmer grip on the pot in his arms, he took a deep breath and announced in a quavering voice, 'You can call me, Bob.'

Bommington's Biscuits

Bommington's Biscuits

The Bommington Biscuit Factory was more than a place which simply produced something sweet to dunk in your tea each day; it was an institution.

Six generations of Bommingtons had carried on a tradition started by the original Oliver Bommington, and each handed it carefully on to the next in line, emphasising the importance of their responsibility in preserving the sacred ritual and art of selecting just the right biscuit or three to go with your afternoon tea.

For nearly two hundred years, devoted workers at the factory had been gathering the best ingredients, weighing, blending, whisking and folding mixtures with the loving care of a diligent mother, and the artisanal skill of a master craftsman. People came from far and wide to purchase a packet of their biscuits. In fact, one packet was seldom enough; it was not unknown for people to leave the adjoining shop with their cars loaded, bulging-to-bursting, with as many goodies as they could stuff into them.

No matter your preference – a Ginger Crumble, a Treacle Snap, a Chocolate Heaven, a Jammy Squidger or a Lemon Cream – Bommington's undoubtedly made it.

More recently, trade had not been quite so brisk. People were starting to buy fewer biscuits and eat carrots or apples instead, as a healthy alternative. Bommington's was not impressed. In fact, Bommington's threatened to be in serious financial trouble.

As the two hundred year anniversary

approached, the Board of Directors met to consider how such an important occasion should be celebrated.

Sitting around the antique table in the ancient panelled offices above the factory, with a plate of the famous Bommington Toffee Twists and Strawberry Snaps arranged on a central platter, Grandpa Charles Bommington, the ageing Chairman, stroked his beard and looked over his glasses at the gathering. His son, now the Director, Rupert Bommington, sat on his right twirling a pen while his grandson, Charles junior, sat on his left mulling over the fact that one day he would be obliged to take over the company himself.

Truth to tell, Charles junior wished he was still back in the garage tinkering with his motorbike where he felt much more comfortable. He was always rather intimidated by these meetings with so many people older than himself, all in their dusty grey suits and with their unwavering focus on the job in hand. It didn't help that life-size portraits of old Oliver Bommington and all his descendants since, were gazing down so seriously from the walls.

Charles junior was still quite new to the business, eager to please but unlike his sisters, Emily and Charlotte who were still at school, quite shy, and better with his hands and engines than with columns of figures and charts of projected annual profits. However, he sat on his hands to be sure he wouldn't fidget, suppressed the hankering for his oily overalls and spanners, and looked earnestly at his grandfather who was poised to begin the meeting.

'Gentlemen,' Grandpa Charles began, not surprisingly since – which was surprising – not a single woman was, or ever had been, a member of the Board; not even great-great-great-great grandmother Amelie, Oliver's wife, who had inspired the entire enterprise with her truly extraordinary Lavender Shortbread and Rhubarb Puffs. She and Oliver had lived next to the factory which they had been forced to set up once it became clear that Amelie's kitchen could no longer keep up with the demand for her beautiful biscuity creations which had started to sell like hot... well... biscuits, back in 1800 and something. The family had occupied that home ever since.

'Gentlemen, I trust you have all been busy with your suggestions for the 200th anniversary of Bommington Biscuits. I see you have many files with you which I also trust are full of ideas.'

Grandpa Charles peered down the table at the weary-looking men and wondered how it was that everyone suddenly seemed so old. Why, he remembered sitting next to Nicholas Trueman at school whenever ago that was; it seemed like just a couple of weeks. And there was faithful Philip Peabody; they used to go fishing together down by the stream at the weekends when they were lads. Arthur Connelly, who was still the undisputed conker champion had his place, and next to him, Johnny Hegarty, who used to go scrumping for apples with him in all the autumns of yesteryear. Charles senior began to ponder whether Johnny could still climb walls and trees with the same feline agility of those happy days...

Realising that he had been daydreaming and that now everyone was looking at him expectantly to lead the discussion, he cleared his throat purposefully and shuffled the papers in front of his own place. A tear seemed to have temporarily blurred his vision so the Chairman, with a small sigh of relief, turned to his son.

'Rupert, why don't you take it from here?'

'Of course, Father...er, sir. Right.' Rupert stopped twirling his pen and put it carefully into his jacket pocket before addressing the men.

'Obviously, this is an important time for

Bommington Biscuits; we have a great deal to celebrate and I'm sure you'll all agree that my Father has led us to this significant moment with the same determination, dedication and drive of all the Bommingtons before him.'

There was a ripple of agreement around the table. Charles junior nodded so enthusiastically that he knocked his own pen onto the floor and sheepishly disappeared to retrieve it. He had given up sitting on his hands and had been practising twirling it like his father, but hadn't yet mastered the skill.

'We cannot ignore the fact that as we embark on a new era here at Bommington's, our customers are buying fewer biscuits these days in order to reduce their sugar intake.' Rupert continued, 'This would spell disaster for us all, and I know that together we will come up with a suitably grand and appropriate means of celebration which will turn people once again to the joy a simple biscuit can bring.'

With so many experienced and clever biscuit brains in the room, you might have thought this would be an easy task. It was not. The suggestions ranged from declaring a public holiday, (something which Bommington's could not possibly do without some kind of Royal Charter and government approval), to distributing free biscuits to every household in the land (something which would certainly trigger immediate financial disaster and possibly the collapse of the entire company).

Nicholas Trueman thought an open day might be the thing, but they had held a memorable one ten years previously with the unhappy outcome of having to throw away large amounts of biscuit mixture thanks to a national flu outbreak, which had caused so much revolting sniffing and sneezing amongst the visitors – who hadn't wanted to miss the wonderful chance to see inside Bommington's of course – that the factory had to be closed for three days to fumigate, disinfect and bleach it back to acceptable operational standards. Nobody wanted to do that again.

Philip Peabody suggested a day out for the staff, preferably somewhere in the country where, perhaps, fishing might be possible...? His idea was rejected since, as both Charles senior, and Rupert pointed out, the idea was to include the community rather than leave them all behind.

Arthur Connelly was quite taken with the idea of a sports day but it didn't have much to do with biscuits; nothing, in fact unless they were to sell some from a branded van.

Johnny Hegarty thought that a rock concert would be the best event ever, if they could book famous bands, build a giant stage in front of the factory and project lights and lasers on to it. His eyes shone with excitement as he described the possibilities: they could sell tickets, make T-shirts, book a fun-fair with a big wheel and a carousel, make candy-floss, invite a circus with acrobats and maybe a zoo with lions and tigers and…

Even Rupert, who was quite a down-to-earth chap, felt himself hypnotised at the grandeur of such a scheme, but was brought back to reality abruptly by a sharp poke in the ribs from his father's walking-stick.

'Er, right… well, some fine ideas, gentlemen. I feel that we are grasping for something excellent; we're on the verge of something stupendous I'm quite sure, but we must not… er, how can I say? Overreach ourselves.' He looked pointedly, yet sympathetically, at Johnny Hegarty whose dreams faded almost instantaneously. 'Keep going though… please. What else do we have?'

The men scratched their heads, doodled on their files, looked out of the window, sucked their teeth, scrunched up their eyes and clicked their tongues with their efforts of concentration. A few of them even scratched each others heads, but it didn't help. The suggestions became increasingly feeble: a raffle; a sponsored silence; a kite-flying competition; a dog show. All very un-biscuity.

Just when they were all giving up hope, Charles junior emerged, slightly ruffled, from his quest beneath the table, triumphantly waving his pen which had got wedged between the floorboards and had taken some time and considerable dexterity to dislodge. He had heard the conversation though and had been struck with his own inspiration.

'I know!' he announced with uncharacteristic confidence in the presence of a room of people whose gazes were now fixed solely on himself. 'Let's have a baking competition that is open to anyone. We can see who can create a new, anniversary biscuit that Bommington's can make for the next 200 years!'

A gasp of admiration now toured the room.

'Why, Charles,' beamed his father, 'what a

brilliant idea!' Charles junior blushed modestly. 'What do you think?' Rupert asked, turning to his own father.

Charles senior wobbled to his feet and looked his grandson straight in the eye. 'My boy, your great-great-great-great-grandfather would be proud of you; and so am I! It's the perfect Bommington's tribute!'

In less time than it takes to munch a Bommington Coffee Crunch, the Board agreed to this excellent scheme, stipulating only that no Board member could take part and, before long, news of the competition was being published and advertised across counties.

There were posters on buses, announcements on the radio and entry instructions on Bommington biscuit wrappers in stores from Land's End to John o'Groats. Almost immediately, young and old began experimenting in their kitchens. There was such a rush to purchase weighing scales, mixing bowls, wooden spoons and baking trays that extra orders had to be rushed through to warehouses far, far away.

Soon the smells of freshly baked biscuits filled the air of towns and villages across the nation as people combined flavours and blended concoctions in the hope of tantalising the palates of the Bommington men, who were poised to judge the outcome.

In the Bommington household itself, the topic of conversation revolved almost entirely around the possibilities of the new Bommington biscuit.

'It really is a fabulous idea,' declared Rupert Bommington at supper one night. 'Charles has undoubtedly saved the day with this one.'

'I thought you didn't like the business,' piped up young Charlotte pointedly to her brother.

'Say, what's that?' spluttered Charles senior from his end of the table. 'Don't like the business?'

Granny Bommington put a calming hand on

her husband's arm while Charles junior squirmed guiltily.

'It's not that I don't like it,' he countered, laughing nervously, 'I mean; who doesn't like a biscuit, right? I just don't understand the details. Engines; that's what I understand.'

'Poo!' exclaimed six year-old Emily. 'It's easy. Put in all the ingredients and out comes a yummy biscuit.'

Mrs Bommington tried to make light of the subject before her father-in-law took offence. 'Well, it's not quite a simple as that Emily, not when you're making them on such a large scale.'

'You weigh the ingredients on the scales before it goes in the oven,' her youngest observed correctly, picking up on the single word before going back to spearing her peas one at a time with her fork. It always took her a terribly long time to eat supper.

'I know,' said Charlotte picking up from her

mother's comment; 'it's called, *scaling up*, Emily. It's what you have to do to make a project work for lots of people and turn it into a business instead of just making enough for your family. You'd have to make hundreds, even thousands of biscuits to make any money from it because you have to buy all the ingredients first. So, you have to get your money back from that before you can even begin to make any for yourself.'

Grandpa Bommington nodded sagely. 'Profit and satisfaction,' he declared, wiping the remains of his meal from his whiskers with a linen napkin embroidered with the Bommington logo.

'Well, that's what we do isn't it?' Rupert chipped in cheerfully, making it sound like a question even though it wasn't.

Charlotte hadn't finished though, 'Yes, but isn't it interesting how different biscuits sell better at different times of year? You can't shift a Lemon Lush in September, but wait until spring and they fly off the shelves.'

Her father raised his eyebrows. 'How on earth do you know that Charlotte?'

'I saw the graphs on your desk when I was looking for some drawing paper for my homework.'

'Hmmmm; I've told you not to go in there young lady.'

'Sorry Dad; it was an emergency.'

'Emergency biscuit; what a good idea,' Charles senior mumbled and gave a big sigh. Granny Bommington's eyes twinkled; she winked at Charlotte meaningfully but, wisely, said nothing.

'I hope someone makes a biscuit that's oil resistant so that I don't have to wash my hands every time I have a tea break in the garage,' said Charles junior as he put his knife and fork neatly together, thanked his Mum politely and headed out to the garage. He was going to spend the evening with his bike, which was currently lying in pieces as he patiently tried to work out from the manual why the engine was making such a strange grinding sound every time he started it up.

The rest of the family cleared up while Charles senior dozed off in his armchair in front of the television mumbling the names of biscuits past and present.

This scenario repeated itself frequently during the coming weeks. There was so much biscuit-making going on around the country that no-one could get away from it. It's all very well to run a business, but most people like to walk away at the end of the day and do something entirely different with their own time. The Bommington family was not at all like those people. Biscuits were in their blood – not literally you understand. My goodness, that would be quite a serious medical problem, I imagine – and their lives revolved around their product.

Mrs Bommington often made up a batch of her

own biscuits ready for the girls to enjoy after school, or for the men to have in their lunchboxes. She would combine the famously well-guarded recipes, coming up with entirely new ones which were quite wonderful. She had, for instance, once made a Snickety Snumble; a cross between a Chocolate Snap and a Raspberry Crumble; delicious! Another time she mixed a Ginger Ring with a Syrup Surprise creating what she called, a Sticky Surring; amazing! They didn't catch on outside her home, mostly because she wasn't allowed into the development or Board meetings and because her husband and father-in-law were too busy in their offices to notice how talented she was.

It's an old story, I'm afraid. Instead, she secretly wrote a monthly column in a progressive ladies magazine under the name of Pamela Spinks, where she channelled her frustration at living in a world run almost entirely by men, and received sack loads of letters of appreciation from other fantastic and capable women. It was quite a job keeping all this under wraps, but Mrs Bommington was nobody's fool and kept her mail in a factory store cupboard to which only she had the key. The firm had so many people working for them that the man in charge of the pay roll assumed Pamela Spinks worked somewhere on the factory floor and never questioned it. Mrs Bommington was a rather clever lady.

The closing date of the competition swiftly approached. Cooks and bakers took off their aprons for the last time, shelved their cook books ancient and modern, shook the flour out of their hair and soaked their baking trays while their ovens, if they could have done so, would have heaved a collective sigh of relief and looked forward to a well-earned rest. Now the bakers just had to submit their wonderful creations and wait.

The day of the judging dawned, clear and bright.

A vast marquee dominated the grounds of Bommington Biscuits and three generations of Bommingtons donned their smartest clothes. Charles senior chose an old-fashioned tail coat with a yellow polka dot bow tie. Rupert had a bespoke, tailored suit in distinguished charcoal, similar to that in which he had got married but which, regretfully, no longer fitted; it was the price he had paid for too many biscuits over the years. Charles junior struggled to be parted from his overalls which he found so very comfortable for all his mechanics but which, he knew, were not acceptable or appropriate Bommington attire for such an important day. He settled on his Sunday best with a striped silk tie which Granny Bommington had given him for Christmas, and which had cost more than any of the other clothes in his entire wardrobe.

Together, the three generations of Bommington men embarked on the judging. As they entered the marquee a cheer went up from the crowds who had gathered beyond the fence where police officers had erected barriers to keep things under control. The excitement was palpable.

Inside the marquee, an overwhelming sight met the eyes of the judges.

Long tables were stacked with plates and platters of cookies and wafers, bars and macaroons as far as the eye could see. And oh, the taste of those little mouthfuls of gorgeousness! There were Blueberry Bakes and Butterscotch Bars; Coconut Crescents and Caramel Crunchies; Digestive Dreams and Date Delights. Some were round, some were square, there were even some triangular biscuits flavoured with Earl Grey tea. Many of the entries were filled with the glorious flavours of fruits and spices; some were full of raisins or nuts or both. They were gooey biscuits and crunchy biscuits; biscuits to melt in your mouth and biscuits to clog your teeth for a fortnight. Some were coloured, many were decorated with sprinkles, or sparkles, or glittering balls, or icing, or chocolate or as many things as their creators could squish onto, or into, their works of art without falling foul of the rules that whatever they submitted, it must be a biscuit and not a cake. Bommington's had never been known for their cakes; they were after all, a biscuit family and a biscuit family they would remain.

By lunchtime the three men were starting to look rather ill, having eaten samples of so many of the entries, yet they had barely started. It was a mammoth task, and on further consideration an announcement was made that the judges, whose decision would be final, would now put aside the entire week to make this important decision as well as bring in the rest of the Board of Directors to help them.

'Why can't *we* try?' asked Emily, peeping through the marquee flap after school. 'It's not fair that only the men taste everything.'

'It's not!' agreed Charlotte vehemently. 'Can't we sneak in Mum? There's heaps of biscuits in there; they'll never even notice.'

Neither girl was wrong but Mrs Bommington, the embodiment of tact and diplomacy, had to tread a fine line between encouraging her daughters' ambitions and sense of justice with a two-hundred-year-old and, to her mind (and that of Pamela Spinks), extremely out-dated tradition.

'The problem is, girls,' she addressed them both while her eyes ranged over the mountains of entries, 'the men need us more than they know.'

Charlotte frowned. 'What do you mean Mum?'

'Well, think about it,' replied her oh-so-sensible mother, 'who goes to the supermarket every week? Who usually does most of the shopping? Who makes sure that morning coffee and afternoon tea isn't forgotten and often ends up clearing it up as well as serving it?'

Emily looked up at her Mum solemnly and

tugged her sleeve. 'You do Mum.'

Mrs Bommington smiled. 'Well, yes in our house I do. But in other families?'

'The women!' Charlotte said with conviction.

'Absolutely,' agreed her mother. 'Now what does that tell you?' It was a question Pamela Spinks had frequently asked her readers.

'Ha!' Charlotte exclaimed triumphantly and, with a determined look in her eye, strode back purposefully towards the house. Mrs Bommington didn't move but smiled a quiet smile to herself while Emily skipped around her like a buzzing fly.

'I don't get it Mum. What does that tell us? Tell me, tell me, tell me.'

She was silenced by an enveloping motherly hug as Mrs Bommington knelt down and pulled her daughter towards herself before delivering a tickle that made Emily giggle so much she could barely breathe.

'It tells us,' whispered Mrs Bommington teasingly, 'that Mums are pretty important.'

The hug she got back let her know that Emily agreed and together they left the marquee and went home to see what was in their own biscuit tin.

The week rolled on and the Bommington men began to think they had tasted all the flavours on earth: liquorice, pumpkin, vanilla, cinnamon, cardamon, apricot, peach, peanut butter, orange, cherry, mint, almond, banana, white chocolate, milk chocolate, dark chocolate, plum... it went on and on. Chocolate-coated, yoghurt-coated, sugar-coated; shortbreads and shortcakes, cookies and fingers with soft centres, jam-centres, crunchy centres, nutty centres, rings without any centre at all. The days wore on and the nights were sleepless as a surfeit of sugar kept them all awake.

By the end of the week disaster loomed: they had each forgotten what they had tasted at the beginning of the week, so were still no closer to finding a winner.

They should really have kept better records, but had been so mesmerised by the quantities of competition entries and the excitement of the moment that they really hadn't kept track properly. The official forms they had prepared for recording each entry had not been filled in properly, if at all, so trying to recall which name, number, and recipe went with each exhibit was virtually impossible. Consequently, the entire competition now threatened to end in disaster and embarrassment for Bommington Biscuits rather than the triumph they had all anticipated.

It was a quarter to five on the final day of judging when the Board, desperate for a winner and loosening their belts, thanks to their collective gluttony and weight gain, came to the end of the tables.

'I think we're in trouble,' groaned Charles

senior, rubbing his protesting stomach and collapsing thankfully into a chair.

'Might have overreached ourselves after all, Father,' admitted Rupert loosening his tie.

There were nods of agreement from the rest of the Board who were all too full to even speak. Clipboards with their half-written comments and smears of jam and chocolate lay scattered on tables and chairs, along with a prodigious number of half-eaten biscuits.

Nicholas Trueman was doubled over and a delicate shade of green. He looked as though he might be sick at any moment. He daren't venture outside in case the police-patrolled crowds realised he wasn't enjoying all this as much as he had hoped.

Philip Peabody had come equipped with a tube of pink indigestion tablets his wife had had the foresight to slip into his jacket pocket after he'd come home on the first day and not been able to eat any supper. He was stuffing them into his mouth two at a time.

Arthur Connelly lay flat on the discoloured grass of the marquee, his chest and ample stomach sprinkled with biscuit crumbs and tell-tale cookies peeping from his pockets. They were, he'd told himself samples of the best ones that he would return to later, but he was now too full to eat them and too muddled to know from which plate he had, literally, pocketed them.

There was no doubt that Johnny Hegarty would be climbing neither trees nor walls in the foreseeable future and not only because of his advancing age. The former apple scrumper had fallen asleep, propped up by one of the marquee poles, one arm wrapped around a tin belonging to a competitor from Halifax and with his mouth half open. The sound of his snores was muffled by the canvas but it was not an attractive sight or sound.

Charles senior tried to button his jacket, but couldn't, and thought how relieved he was that there was nobody around to see what a colossal mess they had made of the whole enterprise which had been such a good idea when his grandson had first suggested it a couple of months ago.

'We're in a pickle,' he concluded, surveying the Board strewn around the last table of entries like skittles felled by a speeding bowling ball. The men groaned, snored or grunted according to their limited ability. Only Charles junior was still standing, resolutely gripping the edge of the table, with a look of intense concentration on his face.

'Hang on!' he intervened grimly, 'There's still one more entry to try.'

'Nooooooo!' came a universal cry from his fellow judges.

Charles junior prised the lid off a rather battered looking lunch box, peered inside and then offered the contents around, nudging Johnny Hegarty

awake with his elbow. Reluctantly, each member of the Board took one and gingerly brought it up to their unwilling mouths.

There was no doubt that these biscuits were different from all the rest. They didn't ooze chocolate or marshmallow; they didn't drip with lurid coloured icing or sticky jam. They didn't smell the same as any of the other biscuits and they didn't taste the same either.

'My goodness!' exclaimed Charles senior, perking up immediately. 'What on earth is this?'

The men all munched in fixated silence for a full minute, expressions of relief creeping slowly across each face. Then all at once, at exactly the same moment of realisation, they all whispered: 'Cheese!'

After all the sickly sweetness of so much sugar, the welcome savoury taste revived their tired taste buds and the spark of dying interest was re-ignited in their eyes.

'These are truly amazing,' breathed Nicholas Trueman, reaching for another.

'Outstanding,' agreed Philip Peabody.

'Remarkable,' nodded Arthur Connelly.

'Exquisite,' sighed Johnny Hegarty.

The men looked at each other and smiled; then they giggled and before long they were laughing and guffawing and slapping one another on the back.

'Gentlemen,' declared Charles Bommington senior, 'I think we have a winner.'

'But Father,' cautioned Rupert, 'can a cheese biscuit truly be a biscuit?'

Charles senior looked doubtful. It was a crucial question for a family who had produced nothing else for the past 200 years. He sniffed reflectively. 'I suppose... technically... it might actually be... a cracker...?' he mused, a shadow of doubt crossing his worried face.

'No!' declared Charles junior forcefully, holding the box and the attention of the members of the

Board, who were temporarily taken aback by another sudden display of his confidence and the new fighting light in his eyes. 'I may know engines better than biscuits, but I know this: we are Bommington Biscuits. We're not Bommington cakes,' he continued, 'not Bommington cookies, not Bommington scones and most definitely not Bommington crackers! But, our family has been making biscuits for two hundred years and there's no-one who can tell us how to do it better. If it has our name on it, it's a biscuit for sure.'

With that he turned the now empty box over and there, clearly written on a sticky label for all to see, was the name of the entrant:

'C Bommington'

'But you can't enter this competition!' spluttered his father, accidentally spraying cheese crumbs all over Johnny Hegarty. 'That would be quite unethical. You're on the Board.'

Charles junior's puzzlement lifted after a brief moment. He smiled knowingly as the realisation dawned on him. He turned and faced the board joyously. 'I didn't make them Dad. Charlotte must have done.'

And that is how Bommington biscuits solved the problem of making their biscuits popular again, as well as celebrating two hundred years of all things biscuity. Not only that, but with Charlotte's inspired help, an entirely new celebratory line of biscuits was born: cheese and apple, cheese and carrot, cheese and pickle, cheese and onion, cheese and herb, cheese and garlic, blue cheese... the list went on, each biscuit more popular than the last; but *never* cheese and sugar!

Since she had clearly shown herself to be a master biscuit-maker the like of whom had not been seen on the premises since great-great-great-great-grandmother Amelie, it wasn't many years before Charlotte left school, studied business and baking and was invited onto the Board of Development and Directors.

No-one was more pleased than Charles junior who was consequently allowed to resign and open his own mechanics business specialising in motorbike engines, except perhaps Pamela Spinks, whose column was soon so popular that she had more than enough material to write a book which became a best seller before you could say, 'Bommingtons Biscuits – Better Than Best'. This was the tagline which now appeared on every packet of the family product.

Mrs Bommington kept her alter-ego a secret but became so busy with this new writing enterprise that she was quite happy to let her eldest daughter and the rest of the family get on with the biscuity side of life. It also meant that one day in the future all those grey, dull portraits of crusty old Bommington men in the Board Room would be joined, at last, by one of a very clever young woman.

The King And i

The King And i

In the Kingdom of Slopingsideways, things were in a rut. They had been in a rut for many years. Over 100 years in fact, during which everyone had been doing all the same things in all the same ways as their parents and grandparents before them.

People cooked their toast over the fire, wrote their letters with ink-filled fountain pens, employed other people to polish their shoes and spent their evenings listening to crackly radios. They took baths once a week in heavy copper tubs, with water which took ages to be heated up in huge saucepans; they had goats grazing in their back gardens, put their wet washing through hand-operated mangles and were just getting used to going to work on a bus instead of on a horse.

This curious state of affairs was the consequence of a freak storm a century before, during which terrible floods cut the Kingdom off from the rest of the world. Being a resourceful people, they had rolled up their sleeves and made the best of the situation by simply getting on with life as they knew it, which was mostly very pleasant, if rather slow. Everyone had time to enjoy watching the sun set, to lean on gates, feed the ducks and daydream.

The only real excitement came around with the Annual Arts Festival held each spring at The Grand Arena. For one entire week tickets could be purchased to watch plays of all sorts: comedies, tragedies, farces and melodramas. You could admire paintings and pottery, tapestries and tableaux; listen to orchestras, brass ensembles and string quartets; attend ballets and poetry readings, and enjoy a multiplicity of creative workshops in etching, sketching and directing.

The much-anticipated finale was always the same: Dame Vera Wobblington, Slopingsideways's famous soprano opera singer, took to the stage for a performance to raise the rafters and the spirits. My, how the people loved her! She followed in the famous footsteps of her mother, Dame Agnes Wobblington, and like her, she regularly enjoyed standing ovations. Every year she received heaps of red roses and bouquets from audiences who were moved to tears by her soaring high notes, and by her passionate embodiment of tragic Italian operatic stories they didn't in the least understand, but found very moving. Some of the notes were so high that the virtuoso had been known to stand on a chair to reach them, and one memorable year she hit a top C note with such vigour that all the exquisite antique chandeliers shattered dramatically. Surprisingly, she was not shredded in the aftermath, even though a million shards of knife-sharp glass fell around her and, after they were replaced with unbreakable replicas, like everyone else in the Kingdom she went back to her normal, slow but pleasant life until the following spring festival.

Meanwhile, the rest of the world beyond Slopingsideways was not stuck in any kind of rut and carried on learning, inventing, changing, and developing steadily. They discovered ready meals, central heating, electric drills, food mixers, jogging, life coaches and computers. These other kingdoms had homes which boasted cars, colour televisions, tumble driers, electric toothbrushes and a host of gadgets which made life a squillion times easier than ever before.

If it hadn't been for young Edgar Naseby, things would probably have stayed as quiet and peaceful in Slopingsideways as they had always been for another 100 years.

One Saturday morning, Edgar was playing

football with his friends in the park on the edge of town. Here, they still used balls made of heavy old leather which needed a jolly good kick to get them moving anywhere at all, especially if it had been raining – that always contrived to make the balls move with the same ease of a wet walrus on a beach. The team were in the final minutes of the second-half, holding a draw, when Edgar, trying to avoid an illegal slide tackle, walloped the ball clean off the pitch and into the undergrowth beyond. He beetled after it, eager to crack on with the game, and discovered the ball had rolled through some nettles (a rather painful discovery to be sure), down a slope and across an odd painted line he had never seen before.

Puzzled, he turned to call his friends, 'Hey! Come and look at this.'

The muddy teams clustered round wondering what the fuss was about. As it turned out, Edgar had stumbled across the old boundary line between Slopingsideways and the next kingdom.

Everyone on Edgar's side of the line had been so busy getting on with life that no one had actually noticed that Slopingsideways was no longer surrounded by flood waters and had, once again, joined up to the rest of the world. The rest of the world had all been so caught up with their new double-glazing and doughnut makers, they had pretty much forgotten their old neighbours and had never bothered to go and check the water levels.

As you can imagine, this new discovery caused quite a stir. Suddenly, important government envoys were dispatched to meet with other national government people and talk about diplomatic relations, national initiatives and partnership programmes. Trade delegations were sent across the border to secure deals and hold talks with all manner of other important people. Before long, exciting new products appeared in the shops: pizza, ready-made pastry, sushi, trainers with velcro fastenings, microwaves, digital watches, hair straighteners, smoke detectors, superglue, remote controls for TVs, photocopiers, CDs... Such a dazzling array of new inventions and merchandise left the people of Slopingsideways quite dizzy with excitement.

In almost no time at all, everyone could accomplish loads more things in half the time they used to, which gave them more time to do a whole bunch of new and exciting things.

Now they had access to skateboards and roller blades, wind surfers, carbon-framed bicycles and fibre-glass canoes for outdoor pursuits; they discovered footballs which didn't break your toes every time you tried to kick them – Edgar and his friends were particularly happy about these. Meals took less time to prepare and there was barely a person or family who didn't enjoy the wonderful DVD films and nature programmes they could watch on their big flatscreen televisions every night.

But, it was universally agreed, the most brilliant new invention of them all was the mobile phone connected to the internet. No one had ever seen anything like it. After a frantic scramble to erect communication towers and electrical masts to establish access to the technology they required, the nation was hooked. Suddenly, magically, here was a gadget that could keep you in touch with everyone all over the world and put entire encyclopaedias of information at your fingertips. It was better than fantastic! Slopingsideways need never worry about being cut off from the rest of the world again.

Now, not only could you let your Mum know that you had to stay behind after school to go to auditions for the end of term play, but business men could send their apologies for missing a meeting rather than just not turn up because they were stuck in traffic.

Yes, Slopingsideways had embraced car travel, and now their tired horses enjoyed more restful days in their paddocks – one of the few places that were phone-free. Relatives could not just call one another, but actually see each other on their screens as they talked. It was a technological revolution.

That was all very well, but most thrilling of all was all the other things these phones could do.

Now you could take photographs and films of everything from your breakfast to your latest sporting achievement; from unique moments, like meeting a celebrity, or being presented with your colossal birthday cake, or proposing to your girlfriend. People played music by one touch of the screen; they could turn their lights and heating on at home while they were sitting miles away in their cars. They could even make the oven turn on so that supper was cooked by the time they got home after seeing friends, or having coffee in the next town, so long as they had remembered to put the dish in the oven that morning of course.

People started using their phones to follow exercise regimes and fashion fads, to order their groceries for home delivery and to find out what the weather was doing on the other side of the world. They asked their phone what time it was, how many times their own heart was beating and obscure questions about mathematics, planetary orbits and Bavarian hummingbirds. Teachers could send entire classes their homework by phone. The council started sending out parking tickets by phone. Really, the car situation was getting rather out of hand.

It was extraordinary; there seemed to be no end to the uses for this little miracle that reached to the ends of the earth yet fitted in a pocket.

But, the most diverting operation of all for the fascinated people of Slopingsideways, was the vast number of games that could be accessed on these little tablets of joy. Old and young became glued to their screens for hours at a time to beat their own personal best scores exploding animated fruit, or squashing aliens, or solving increasingly difficult levels of complicated quizzes and puzzles. It was all very jolly. From the palace to the pavement, everyone was glued to their screens.

And this is when it all started to go horribly wrong.

The problem was, that the more people played on their phones, the less they talked to each other face-to-face, and consequently, the less work got done. Soon offices were buried in mounds of filing; letters went unanswered and bills didn't get paid; roadworks became a nightmare because people were always falling in holes that had been dug and not filled in because the workmen were busy navigating a particularly difficult level on their phone. Usually the ones who fell into the holes had also been on their phones and hadn't noticed the lack of solid pavement ahead.

Customers in restaurants waited hours for their meals because the chefs were busy discovering new ways to flambé their rhubarb or dress an artichoke, referring to some clever cooking gizmo provided by their phone. The waiters had nothing to serve, so used the time to post photos of their feet or the customers who wore funny clothes.

Court judges stopped turning up to work and just sent their verdicts on important cases to the courts by phone. The army idled their time away playing army-type strategy games using their screens, because their senior officers were all catching up on world history on their phone Apps. Teachers forgot to come out of the staff room to do their teaching as they discovered that education techniques, standards, methods and curriculums – or was it curricula? – in other Kingdoms had all raced ahead of their own and they were desperately trying to find out via their phones how to use an interactive white board, and what exactly the third form needed to know about the life cycle of newts.

Farmers who had spent their lives milking their cows by hand suddenly needed to know how to use machines for the job, and how to check the daily output of each cow in order to report to the International Agricultural Standards Committee, a group they had never even heard of prior to the phone revolution.

Shops began to lose business because the customers evaporated when they found they could order everything from a pint of milk to a new raincoat, or half a ton of topsoil from the comfort of their own homes using their phones. Half of the shop assistants and retail managers didn't notice because they were too busy watching cute videos of kittens, or laughing at speeded up loops of people falling off things on their phones.

Things were no better in the Royal Palace. Yes,

the Kingdom of Slopingsideways did indeed have a King, and a Queen. The Queen, on this occasion, was not amused. She had no time for phones and didn't care who knew it.

'Ghastly waste of time!' she announced when the King had been presented with one in a special silver box tied with a purple ribbon. 'Why on earth would you need such a thing?'

She had been very happy with the way things were before what she regarded as Edgar Naseby's unfortunate discovery; she enjoyed a gentle pace of life and took every opportunity to lean on a gate or watch the sun set. However, she was also given a phone in a fancy box too, and, because she had been well brought up, managed to say, 'Thank you' politely before stuffing it behind one of several large hat boxes in her Royal wardrobe and not giving it any further thought.

The King, quite unperturbed, loved his deluxe phone and used it for all sorts of things. He could send his wife a message to let her know he wouldn't be attending afternoon tea as he was still busy with a foreign dignitary at the other end of the palace. He could inspect the troops via the camera on his phone rather than have to squeeze into his official uniform, which was several sizes too small these days. He didn't have to turn up on the parade ground at all, and so avoided having to pretend his trousers weren't chaffing as badly as they were in several very awkward places. He was even able to check up on the security of the Crown Jewels at the touch of a phone button which gave him real-time footage of the Royal safe.

He had also discovered a particularly amusing game in which he blasted coloured dragons to gain points and could earn extra 'crowns' at each level which then gave him super-powerful blasters to use in the next level. He was entranced. The game had been specifically designed just for him by the IT phone whizzes in the adjoining Kingdom as a diplomatic gift.

The Queen meanwhile, remained baffled. She enjoyed talking to people who were in the same room rather than fiddling around with buttons and screens and, try as she might, she couldn't understand everyone's fascination with this new gadget. She had never worried if her husband didn't turn up for afternoon tea anyway since it had always meant she could eat his piece of cake herself and there was no one she had to share the scones with either; an entirely satisfactory state of affairs.

The Prime Minister had taken to sending recordings of himself giving weekly updates on what had happened in Parliament, rather than turning up for an actual meeting at the Palace. The Lord Chamberlain spent his time working on an App which would predict which uniform would be needed by which monarch for any given occasion, and was attempting to programme it to create an interactive wardrobe. This meant he was never around to do the Lord Chamberlainey things he was supposed to be doing. Even the cook was deciding which meal to prepare for the Royal dining room based on what her phone told her was being cooked in other palaces around the world.

Things came to a head in the days running up to the Spring Festival.

It had been decided that this year the Kingdom must make more effort to produce something on a much larger scale now that the national borders were once again open and a much wider audience from the surrounding kingdoms was expected. The Grand Finale should be bigger, better, more lavish and far more truly grand than ever before. There would be fireworks, an acrobatic fly-by preformed by a newly skilled aircraft squadron and ceremonial cannons to celebrate Slopingsideways's return to international life.

All this required a great deal of organisation, as you can imagine; and so a punishing schedule of important (and mostly bossy) people was drawn up, most of whom were due to make their requests at the palace before leaping into action to make sure there were enough chairs, refreshments, parking attendants, spare light bulbs and toilet rolls.

Everything was to bear the crest of the Royal household, which meant that the King and Queen had to give their approval to every little detail. This was a lot to ask and the whole process would have been much smoother if the Lord Chamberlain and his staff could have done the job. As it was, they carried on gaining eye-wateringly high scores while competing with one another in a new game they had just discovered on their phones, solving riddles.

Every day new delegations formed a queue through the Royal hallways, waiting for their turn to be granted an audience with the Monarchs. The Queen was ready, waiting and eager to get started. The King however, was not; he was, as you may have guessed, very busy on his phone.

On Monday he was late because he was learning about Abyssinian pottery; on Tuesday he was delayed watching a nail-bitingly close game of tennis which he had missed because the Queen had insisted on getting him fitted for a new pair of trousers at the same time that the match was actually played. On Wednesday, the Royal equerry found him sitting by the ornamental pond, thoroughly transfixed by the latest report on updates in textile manufacturing now being introduced in the kingdom. Thursday saw him losing track of time in the Royal stables while analysing horseshoe sizes and shapes on his phone, and comparing them with the ones being used in other Royal households around the world.

The Queen became increasingly irritated with

this, not least because she knew there was still heaps to do, but she also felt it was very rude to the people who were waiting for them.

Friday was the last straw.

She had been twiddling her thumbs, waiting for the King for almost three hours, and doing her best to reassure the women's Cake-And-Pastry-Making Guild that they could indeed serve chocolate, coffee and indeed toffee gateaux at the festival if they wished and for as many hours as they wished, just so long as there was a clear note of the ingredients on each one, in case anyone had a nut allergy. She had a pile of papers all awaiting her husband's stamp of approval and finally, having already sent a dozen members of staff to track him down, and in infuriated desperation, she excused herself from the room and went to look for him herself.

'Arthur!' she scolded when she finally found him sitting on his old school books in the attic frantically blasting yet more digital dragons. 'This is ridiculous and it has to stop. Now! Our entire Arts Festival cannot be, and will not be, ruined by these terrible phones. I've had enough!'

Quick as a whistle, she grabbed the phone from his hands in a most un-royal kind of way, plunged it into the deep pockets of her dress and marched the King back to his duties. He was not a happy man at that moment, but what could he do? He had a feeling that his wife was right and that he had been un-kingly himself in neglecting his duties.

Feeling rather embarrassed, and apologising to the hordes of people he had kept waiting, he spent the rest of the day stamping papers, agreeing with his wife and listening to arrangements and plans until his head throbbed.

By the time afternoon tea came around he had perked up a bit; the prospect of the Arts Festival had reminded him of what a fabulous event it was, how much he enjoyed it every year and what a great Kingdom he had the good fortune to rule.

Reluctantly, he agreed with the Queen that everyone must switch off their phones at the planned events, or have them confiscated. Drastic action, but they would do it if they had to. Nothing should be allowed to distract people from the superb seven days of excellence which had been planned with so much care.

Indeed, all too quickly, the Festival began and the week passed in a whirr of excitement and all-round artistic wonderfulness. Actors acted with passion and drama; dancers danced their socks and occasionally their shoes, clean off; painters painted extraordinary pictures with watercolours, oils, pastels, raw eggs and even, symbolically, with mud from multiple Kingdoms. Sculptors sculpted with vigour and chisels; jewellers exhibited bespoke pieces which sparkled like stars and provoked gasps of wonder from festival goers.

Edgar Naseby and his friends particularly enjoyed an exhibition on, *The history of football in one hundred black and white photographs*, mostly because their own Saturday team was pictured above a caption recording their discovery of the old Slopingsideways boundary line. His Mum enjoyed it too and felt very proud (although it did interrupt her research into ethnic knitting which she had been discovering at home on her phone).

The day of the Grand Finale arrived at last. It would be the highlight of the entire week, the most splendid concert the Kingdom had ever heard, with hordes of visitors from other kingdoms packed into the performance area of the historic arena.

The theatre was ready: the lights were bright, the stage was polished, the red velvet seats were brushed, the programmes were piled high and the microphones tested.

Dame Vera Wobblington squeezed herself into a

dress with so many sequins that the dress fitters needed to wear sunglasses while they scurried around making their last minute adjustments. She gargled with disinfectant, sucked throat lozenges and practiced her scales at half volume in order to ensure her voice was in peak condition for the performance. It promised to be a spectacular and memorable event in every way.

It is true that the audience filed in with a certain amount of grumbling. There had been an unexpected amount of resistance by some to turning off their phones, especially from those from other kingdoms. Although they felt honoured to be there for such an historic occasion, the reality was that the choice of arias and operas was somewhat challenging for them and not quite to their own taste. Without connection to the Kingdom of Slopingsideways, they had only recently heard of Dame Vera Wobblington and knew nothing of her famous mother and very little of the honour in which they were both held by the country. Truthfully, they would have preferred a modern rock concert from a popular group, and so had planned to secretly while away the time on the latest phone game which required finding hidden objects in a picture, so they were somewhat put out that they would now have to give Dame Vera their full attention.

The lights dimmed; people 'Ssshhh'-ed each other, stopped rustling their sweet wrappers, cleared their throats hurriedly and settled into their velvet seats, ready to be transported by the voice of the famous singer. Everyone who had just sat down had to stand up again as the King and Queen were escorted into the Royal Box by uniformed gentlemen wearing white gloves and ceremonial uniforms, while an unseen orchestra played the National Anthem. People nudged one another excitedly and then sat and settled themselves all over again.

The excitement was at fever-pitch. The plush curtains parted and the star glided onto the stage as though she was on wheels. It was mesmerising.

Everything went according to plan: Dame Vera Wobblington was magnificent! Her voice was rich and smooth, clear and true; even the listeners who usually leaned towards other types of music, found themselves enchanted by her beautiful interpretations of the programmed pieces. So much so, that the interval seemed like rather a rude interruption, and apart from the usual surge towards to the toilets (as you know, there are never enough of these in any theatre), people couldn't wait to return to their seats. Even the refreshment bar remained fairly empty.

The King and Queen were served delicious and exotic fruit sorbet ice creams in the Royal Box, and they took the opportunity to remark to each other that all the hard work prior to the Festival had been well worth it to reach this moment of international success.

The second-half began, and this would be the climax of the entire Festival week. The sound of the orchestra rose and swelled in time with each piece, interpreting the emotion of the composer and reflecting the intensity of Dame Vera's passion as she told musical stories and acted out tales of courage, treachery and love. The audience smiled; the audience cried. People were stirred, moved, excited and shaken by the effect of this one astonishing voice; truly it was – she was – extraordinary.

What they didn't know was that the illustrious Dame had been building up to something even she had never done before in public. She was going to finish with a specially commissioned piece which would include singing the highest note – the A note above the topmost C – that a person had ever managed to reach.* It was a hugely

---

* *The A above 'top C' was considered, 'a note so high it has never been sung before',* until soprano Audrey Luna hit it superbly in her operatic performance at the Met Opera in New York in November 2017. (*https://www.nytimes.com/2017/11/07/arts/music/metropolitan-opera-high-note-exterminating-angel.html* accessed 12.04.22)

ambitious idea and would guarantee her place in musical history for ever, as well as being a fitting end to this important year of new national beginnings.

Taking a step forward and adjusting her stance, Dame Vera took several deep breaths that threatened to burst the seams on her sparkly dress, and began.

It was a piece that would build up in speed, volume and pitch to that all important note. Lesser performers would have thought better of it and simply sung a lower harmony, but that was not Ms Wobblington's style. As she approached the crucial moment, she allowed herself to take in the sweep of the whole theatre: the riveted listeners whose hearts she had captured with her songs; the classical architecture; the heat of the spotlights; the feel of the stage through her leather-soled shoes; the flicker of nerves in her own stomach; the presence of Royalty and the expectation of a stunning finale which she would deliver with previously unknown flair.

She had never felt so alive.

With excitement rising in her own mind, she deliberately caught the eye of the conductor to allow herself an extra breath and then, with every fibre of her being and every vocal chord stretched to capacity she soared to the highest of high notes and lingered there for just a fraction of a second.

It was enough; and it was a triumph!

The unbreakable chandeliers flickered but, fortunately, neither went out nor crashed to the floor.

A sound like the crack of thunder, the splitting of the earth, the shattering of glass and the crash of a thousand rock falls however, rent the air beyond the theatre. It went completely unnoticed inside the theatre where the audience was on it's stomping feet clapping and shouting, whistling and cheering which successfully disguised those

noises which had come from far beyond the reverberating walls. Almost every other window and piece of glass in the Kingdom shuddered with the onslaught of that A note for a week; trees shivered and buildings trembled.

The newly installed phone masts however, did not fare so well.

Every single mast and satellite dish in the kingdom had blown a fuse or crashed to the ground, or both; unable to stand in the face of sound waves which ripped them from their very foundations.

Everyone's phone was dead.

It didn't matter how many times they turned them off and on again, shook them, stabbed at the keys with angry fingers or yelled at them; there was just no signal at all. This was discovered only when the audience finally left the venue and tried to access their phones again, even while the last flowers that had been thrown onto the stage were still being gathered up into a massive bouquet for Dame Vera.

Thanks to the degree to which everyone had come to rely on their phones, this presented a massive national crisis which was brought before Parliament the very next day. Visitors, of course, had returned to their neighbouring countries and picked up their local signals with ease so that problem was solved. But, across Slopingsideways there was an outcry. Simultaneously, there was also a lot more time for most people to return to the tasks that had been so sorely neglected for the past few months.

The Government announced that it would take a while to mend everything and so, somewhat reluctantly, everyone went back to the shops again, letters were answered, papers were filed and even the King had no choice but to return to the chores of Royalty and become reacquainted with the joys of afternoon tea.

In fact, before long it became clear that the disaster had turned into a very helpful wake-up call. A ray of hope and understanding spread across the land as everyone realised that their phones had been slowly, subtly, sucking the life and pleasure out of their lives.

Families who had previously had their noses stuck to their phone screens went back to playing board games, talking and laughing together again; Edgar and his friends took to the football pitch once more, albeit with a much-improved football; restaurants became places of chatter and buzz; offices became productive again and people felt that they were being heard and valued once more.

This left the Government in turmoil; what on earth should they do? They had assumed that all the technological paraphernalia would simply have to be mended or replaced but now they weren't sure whether that's what they, or anyone else, actually wanted.

In a flash of inspiration, the Prime Minister sought an audience with the Queen who, he knew, seemed to have a far better grasp on things than most of his advisors. He arrived just in time for fresh crumpets and hot tea, which reminded him what he had been missing all these weeks by relying only on his on-line updates.

'What do you advise, Ma'am?' he inquired, boldly helping himself to another crumpet slathered with melted butter.

The Queen had actually been giving this a great deal of thought before his arrival. She was relieved that the King was no longer hiding away blasting his wretched cyber dragons, but she was well aware that in order to operate as a modern nation, Slopingsideways could not give up the clever phones completely, or they would simply be left behind again. Tempting as that was, she did not think that was really a good solution for the people she and her husband not only ruled, but loved and cherished.

She furrowed her brow and regarded her Prime Minster, as butter trickled messily down his chin. Automatically, she handed him a napkin and he managed to blush and dab his face at the same time.

'There is no question in my mind,' she said decidedly, 'that these pesky phones are a requirement of modern living. However, I think that we have people clever enough to help us engage with them in a healthier, more inclusive, more Slopingsidewaysey-kind of way.'

The Prime Minister raised his eyebrows wondering what was coming next.

'Prime Minister, I strongly suggest that we change the settings on accessing information and games on these undoubtedly clever, and ingenious gadgets. Is there, perhaps a way we can all enjoy those games on certain days, or weekends, or public holidays, in a way which will still give us time with one another, to read books, to play games, to relax and enjoy all the delights of our Kingdom and all the ordinary but wonderful things that life offers us? We don't want to control or censor, but we all want to retrieve some aspects of our unique lives again.'

The Prime Minister cleared his throat as he considered the wisdom of his Queen, eyed the remaining crumpet hopefully, and nodded slowly as if he had been having the very same thought. He had not.

And so it was, by recommendation and order of the Queen, that the Kingdom of Slopingsideways cautiously embraced again the advances of technology. This time however, they chose to take their place in the ever-changing world still able to lean on gates, feed the ducks, daydream, and enjoy a truly remarkable Annual Festival.

Dame Vera Wobblington became a travelling international star, although she never tried for that top A note again. And, every now and again, on slow weekends, the King could still be found blasting virtual dragons on his phone and hoping to beat his highest score before it was time for tea.

The Red Dragon Of Wales

The Red Dragon Of Wales

There are some who say that dragons don't exist.

Dragons, they believe, are creatures who only appear in fables and myths and that one would never meet one on the way to the supermarket or when going to the park. I am not so sure. Perhaps you have just caught a glimpse of one in the distance, frolicking on the beach or disappearing into the woods yourself, and thought your mind must be playing tricks on you. But what if it wasn't?

I say that just because you haven't seen such a thing doesn't mean that it doesn't exist. I have never seen a giant jellyfish, a winning lottery ticket or a meteor shower; I have never clapped eyes on the Prime Minister's cat, the Queen's lawn-mower or a duck-billed platypus, but I am told that such things are as real as the nose on your face.

Many years ago, of course, there were far more dragons than you will find today and most of them lived in Wales, a country of such greenness it will dazzle your eyes. The hills are lush and covered in flocks of contented sheep who spend their days grazing the emerald-coloured grass. Of course, it's the sheep that used to make the place so attractive to dragons because, like you and I, they have to eat something and a simple sandwich just doesn't do it for them. Or at least, that didn't used to be the case.

The friendly dragons could be called upon by the good people of Wales to help light the coal or wood in their fireplaces if it had become damp, which it often did. This was before central heating was invented of course. A sheep in annual repayment was considered a small price to pay.

Dragons are also able to fly, which meant that they could travel all over the country without clogging up the roads and making a nuisance of themselves. The sheep stayed in their fields keeping a weather eye out for hungry dragons and retreating to the hedge lines, where they were more protected, should any be spotted.

Dragons are also notorious – which is not as nice as being famous because it means they have a rather a bad reputation about something – notorious for being greedy, not so much for pork pies, or chocolate or doughnuts, but for treasure.

Years ago, Wales used to have gold hidden away beneath the hills and whatever the dragons hadn't found was mined by hard-working local people. Nowadays it is very rare and precious, which is perhaps why it has been used for the royal family's wedding rings since 1923.

If you look back into the old stories you will discover that dragons like to make their homes in caves where they store their gold and jewels in huge heaps, and then they sleep on the top of it all so that no-one else can come and steal it from them. It sounds terribly uncomfortable to me, but then I am not a dragon. Dragons must like it because they hibernate there during the cold months when ice and snow cover the Welsh hills.

Long ago, people living in the western valleys of Wales were frequently snowed in and, very sensibly, would keep a shovel by the front door in case the soft flakes piled up overnight and they couldn't get out in the morning.

Once the dragons were awakened by the warming, watery spring sunshine, they would open one eye slowly and stretch in much the same way you do on a weekend or at the start of the school holidays and, like you, one of the first thoughts that would stir in their heads would be:

I'm hungry. You probably put on your cosy dressing gown and slippers and pad downstairs to make some toast, but a dragon – at least in the old days – would have only one meal on his or her mind: sheep. There were no vegetarian dragons in those days and, like the big cats of Africa, they were at the top of the food chain.

Heaving themselves off their treasure piles and scattering jewels and coins in all directions, a dragon would emerge stumbling into the daylight, blinking and squinting before flying high into the sky, relishing the warmer air rushing past their knobbly faces, and scanning the fields below for sheep. I won't frighten you with horrible descriptions of what happened next, but you must know that dragons have big feet with enormous, sharp claws that can pick things up – like sheep – very easily, and carry them long distances if they need to. If a dragon thinks it is mealtime then that is exactly what they think about and exactly what they do and that's that, but they have never been known to kill sheep for sport; that is the sort of senseless things humans might do, but not dragons.

When your great-great-great-grandmother was no higher than my knee, she would have been told about dragons; especially if she was fortunate enough to have lived in Wales. I believe mine was, so perhaps this is how I know this story and can tell it to you now.

1962 was the coldest winter in living memory; however, even that was not as cold as the one in 1740, which was the year the dragons really came into their own. This is what happened:

Away up in the corner of north-west Wales, farmer Idris Jones had woken early one late December morning just before Christmas, to an odd, rather eerie light filling his bedroom. He was always an early riser of course, as farming folk are, but venturing out of his warm bed leaving his wife to sleep a little longer, he shuffled to the icy window and peered through the shutters into the morning gloom.

The peculiar light alerted him to the unfortunate discovery that what had begun as a light sprinkling of snow when they had fallen asleep must have become a raging storm overnight leaving snow so deep that their sheep were completely covered and were now nowhere to be seen. All he could see in the strange morning light was snow, as far as the eye could see, which wasn't actually very far at that time of day.

You have heard of 'a blanket of snow' I'm sure; Idris Jones saw exactly that. Gates and hedges had disappeared; the world looked like one giant milk-covered field.

With a shout of alarm, Idris realised that all of his sheep must now be lying underneath the piles of cold snow. He hadn't brought them in from the fields and now they would freeze to death if they

weren't rescued. There was no time to lose.

Woken by his cries, Betty, his wife and their twin daughters Bronwen and Cerys tumbled out of their beds pulling on shawls and thick stockings to ward off the sharp coldness as they rushed to see what the shouting was about.

'Quick girls!' their father instructed, 'You'll need to help me this morning. Look now, the flock is in trouble and the skies look ready to throw another heap o'snow our way before the morning's over!'

The sisters ran back to their room to gather as many clothes as they could find in the pale morning light. In those days girls didn't wear trousers and had to rely on layers of thick old-fashioned (and often scratchy) bloomers and petticoats to keep themselves warm.

Their mother clambered down the rickety stairs, carrying a candle to light the way, where she lit the oil lamps and set about brewing some tea and a pot of her famous porridge so her family had something hot in their stomachs before facing the frozen world; but Idris brushed past her.

'No time! We must move fast this morning or we'll be too late, my precious.'

So saying, he flung on his biggest sheepskin coat, jammed a hat on his head and unhooked the long red scarf Betty had knitted him last Christmas, winding it around his neck until he was as trussed as the Yuletide turkey, with only his dark eyes glittering like coals beneath the brim of his hat.

'Hurry girls!' his concerned but muffled voice was scarcely heard, but Bronwen and Cerys were already sitting on the flagstone floor, swathed in flannel bloomers and as many petticoats as they had been able to find, lacing their boots and struggling with gloves and extra shawls. Together, they heaved open the old, wooden door, grabbed a crook apiece – a crook is a special shepherd stick with a hook for a handle – and stumbled into the white world.

What a sight met their eyes! They couldn't tell field from farmyard, barn from byre. All the world was grey and white. The menacing sky was filled with slate-coloured clouds full of yet more snow, which scudded so close to the ground it seemed they might reach out and touch them. The freezing air crept around them like a cape, it's fingers finding gaps between their clothing and sending shivers through their bodies.

But these were no ordinary girls. Other farming families had clicked their tongues sadly and shaken their heads in commiseration when Idris and Betty's girls were born. The valley people accepted the old-fashioned lie that every farmer must want sons: strapping lads who would grow big and strong, who could toss hay bales all day long, pull a sheep from a ditch with the ease of shelling a pea from its pod, and shake off the demands of a long day of hard labour in the relentless rain and cold for which Wales is also known. But Idris knew differently; he knew that a girl can also show great strength of body, mind and spirit and the fact that the good Lord had seen fit to give him two such girls was a source of joy to him. He had never regretted their lack of sons, and the girls had proven their worth through all their eight seasons, learning the skill of shepherding a flock, recognising signs of bluetongue, redgut, and liver-fluke diseases, rescuing wanderers from ditches and gullies, helping at shearing and lambing seasons, as well as going without sleep to nurture the helpless bundles if the silly mothers rejected their offspring.

They hadn't cried or wailed or screamed the first time they saw a dragon either. They understood the tricky relationship between sheep farmers and dragons and accepted it as part of life. Cerys in particular, was always badgering her father for stories of dragons which, truth to tell, he rather enjoyed himself, especially the legend of Emrys, the famous red dragon of Wales last seen, so it was said, within sight of their very own farm.

No, Idris had never wasted time wishing for boys; in any case, the two girls were as good as three sons any day.

Now, he gritted his teeth, gripped a shovel in one hand and his shepherd's crook in the other and began the grim job of thrusting it through the snow drifts, hoping to hear the sound of a sheep he could dig out and save.

Bronwyn and Cerys began the same job though, of course, their shepherdess crooks had been made in proportion to their height so were much smaller than their father's. Unperturbed by that, they poked the snow and called out hoping the sheep would hear their familiar voices and bleat to let them know where they were. Soon they were rewarded by the faintest of sounds, and the girls began to dig frantically at the snow, intent on rescuing the poor animal.

It was tiring work and very quickly the cold vanished as they warmed to the task and young arms and legs pushed down through the frozen carpet around them. Cerys turned her crook, hook-side-down, and began to feel her way to a sheep she was certain was there. Sure enough, though she could see nothing, the crook latched itself around a sheep's leg and together the girls carefully hauled out the protesting animal. Whipping some rope from her pocket, Bronwen looped it around the confused sheep and pulled her back to the house. Together the girls bundled the first animal into the stable block and pulled warm hay around her.

'That's fine work, girls,' called their mother, now emerging from the farmhouse also swathed in layers of clothes, a scarf around her head and carrying a pot of hot mash. Realising that her porridge wasn't going to be eaten that morning

Betty had swiftly adapted it to make something hot for the poor sheep. She had already placed piles of rags into the outhouse to use as makeshift towels so she could give the animals a good rub down as each one was brought in.

Almost immediately, Idris emerged from the grey dawn with a sheep under each arm which he dumped unceremoniously next to the first and, nodding to his wife, turned and retraced his steps to begin again leaving her to continue her tasks; the twins scampered after him.

It was long, slow work which drained the strength from man and girls alike.

Folk have always been made of sterner stuff in Wales than some other parts of the world, and they have a strength of will much admired elsewhere, but this morning energy ebbed out of them with every plunge of the crook and every shovel of snow. Before midday it was clear they must take a breather.

The sun refused to break through, so it was almost as hard to see where they'd worked as where they needed to extend the search. Seventeen sheep were now safe and snug inside, apparently none the worse for their experience. It seemed that the covering of snow had, indeed, worked just like a blanket, trapping the warmer air beneath it and keeping the worst effects of an icy night away.

Nevertheless, the family were still well aware that too much delay would threaten every sheep still stuck out in the fields. A decimated flock would mean a disastrous loss of livelihood and no food on their table. Their own survival was at stake.

'Come on, girls,' instructed their father after a swift lunch of hot soup and rough bread. 'there are still sheep buried out there.' Their fingers had barely thawed out, but Bronwyn and Cerys made no complaint as, refastening their clothing, they headed out again.

Two hours and eight more sheep later, and the

sisters were just about at the end of their strength.

'If only we could have some help,' Bronwyn gasped, tugging another sheep to safety.

'Oh Bron,' Cerys sympathised, watching her breath make misty clouds as she spoke. 'I wish we could too, but everyone must be away searching out their own flocks. We'll just have to do our best.'

So saying, she staggered backwards and fell up to her waist in snow, knocked over by the rescued and eager sheep which ran home unescorted, relieved to hear the bleats of it's companions from down in the yard.

Bronwyn helped her sister up and, hands on hips, looked around.

'I can't even see Da anymore. He must be over in the next pasture somewhere.'

Cerys joined her, panting and squirming as melted snow soaked through her sleeves. Suddenly her brave words seemed weak and feeble; she felt overwhelmed by the size of the task.

'Bron; I'm not sure we can do this.'

'We have to!' declared her sister forcefully. 'We've no choice Cerys, you said so yourself; come on!'

Urging her sister to resume the search, Bronwyn picked up her crook and began wearily stabbing at the thick snow. But Cerys stood, chewing her lip thoughtfully.

'There must be a way…'

'Cerys! Come on! We can't let Da, down and I can't do this on my own.'

'I know; but…' Cerys was looking out beyond where the hedge used to be visible.

'Come *on,* Cerys!' Bronwyn pulled at her sister's coat.

'No, wait!' Cerys's eyes were alight with purpose again. 'I have an idea!'

Picking up her skirts she plunged into the snow of the upper field, calling behind her, 'Come on,

Bron. Hurry!'

With a roll of her eyes Bronwyn clambered through the drifts as best she could to catch up.

'Where are we going? We can't leave Da,' she pleaded. 'What about the rest of the sheep?'

But Cerys surged onwards beyond the first field, beyond the second and beyond the lane beyond that, though you wouldn't have recognised any of that since the landscape was still one vast snowy plain.

Neither spoke for a while, concentrating on the effort required to take every step when their boots sank so deep it was hard to pull them out again to take another giant step. They plodded like that for a good twenty minutes before Bronwyn paused to catch her breath.

'Where are we going?'

'You'll see!'

There was no stopping Cerys, even when she slipped down a bank and into the river valley beyond. That was the only clue to where they found themselves.

'I don't think we should be here,' whispered Bronwyn, her eyes as big as saucers.

'Nonsense!' exclaimed her sister. 'This is exactly where we should be. We're going to get some help.'

'Cerys! We can't… We mustn't…'

Her sister whirled round to face her and Bronwyn could tell that Cerys's chin was sticking our determinedly even under all those wrappings.

'We can and we will.' Straightening her shoulders she continued, 'We're going to ask the dragon to help us!'

Cerys had remembered the story of the famous red dragon who lived beneath the ruins of King Vortigern's ancient castle which was on the edge of their father's farmland. It was, after all, he who had told it to her several summers before. Here, where in spring the River Glaslyn ran so prettily, she hoped to find him and wake him from his slumbers.

It was a bold plan, for rousing a dragon from his winter sleep should never be undertaken lightly; you never know how grumpy any animal might be and if it's one who breathes fire as well, then anything might happen.

Bronwyn tumbled down the slope to stand with her sister. She didn't understand how a dragon could help, red or otherwise, but she wasn't one to turn and run at the first hint of danger. Reaching for her sister's gloved hand and summoning their courage, together they walked to the edge of the frozen river where Cerys pulled the shawl from her face and called:

'Emrys!'

Her voice sounded feeble in the cold air. She called again, louder this time, 'Emrys!'

The hills swallowed the sound and the eerie quietness settled again.

'Do you think he's in his cave?' Cerys whispered.

'Don't ask *me*,' came the surprised reply, 'I never

knew we even *had* a dragon so close to home!'

'Come on!'

Cerys pulled her sister along towards a copse of trees where shadows lay like silent threats. Creeping forward they saw the entrance to a cave, its mouth black as night; it seemed to breathe hostility.

The girls looked at one another, taking in the enormity of what they were about to do. Stamping the snow from their boots and nodding grimly, they took a deep breath and felt their way forward. A damp-smelling passage turned sharply to the left and immediately a dull glow from somewhere cast just enough light to show the way.

In barely two minutes the sisters found themselves dazzled, in a cave where light sparkled from every surface reflecting from urns and pots, coins and brass-bound chests. This was indeed a treasure trove and there, sprawled across it all was a large, red dragon.

It is all very well to hear stories of strange creatures and even, if you are very fortunate, to study pictures of them in books from the comfort of your own home. To come face to face with one in real life is quite a different experience, even for the bravest soul. This one was clearly sleeping soundly; two puffs of smoke emerged regularly from it's nostrils indicating the regular breathing of a heavy sleeper. Emrys, for that is indeed who he was, lay on his tummy, wings folded neatly along his back, a contented expression on his scaly, scarlet face.

Conscious of the emergency that needed attention back in the fields, the girls now faced the dilemma of how to wake the creature up.

'Excuse me,' Cerys began politely, 'hello...?'

She was interrupted by the most terrific din which sounded like crashing saucepans and was astonished to see Bronwyn perched on top of an old chest bashing two golden vases together as if her life depended on it.

Almost purple in the face and breathing heavily she showed no fear as she shouted, 'Hey! Dragon! Wake up! It's time to wake up!'

Sure, thought Cerys uneasily, *she could wake the dead with this noise.*

She hoped such a vigorous alarm call wouldn't anger the dragon before they'd had a chance to ask for his help.

As they watched, one large golden eye flicked open and closed again. Bronwyn slithered noisily down a pile of coins setting off a small avalanche of treasure as she rejoined Cerys. The eye opened again more slowly and stared at them without expression.

'Are you all right?' Cerys enquired.

'Well, I thought…' Bronwyn began.

'Not you; the dragon,' Cerys corrected her. 'Emrys, sir; so sorry to wake you, but we need your help'

The dragon didn't stir.

'Really, it's quite urgent.'

'MR DRAGON,' Bronwyn bawled, 'you need to WAKE UP NOW!!!!'

She lifted the vases again, about to resume her clanging, but it was unnecessary.

The dragon rolled onto his side, sending coins sliding towards them, so he could see them better and lifted his big head. His expression was no longer contented and there appeared to be sparks dancing threateningly around his mouth, which revealed sharp teeth as he spoke blearily.

'You dare to disturb a dragon?' he enquired slowly in his gravelly voice.

'Why yes, Emrys sir. On this occasion I think you'll find it was necessary.'

Cerys curtsied as she spoke, not quite sure of the etiquette when addressing a dragon who might eat you at any second.

The dragon frowned, if such a thing is possible.

'How do you know my name?' he asked, not

unreasonably.

'Well, sir, my Da told me stories about you when I was wee-er than I am now. He told me of the famous red dragon, Emrys, who sleeps in this valley and who once helped Merlin before the time of King Arthur. We farm over yonder and see dragons sometimes, but they're usually a green colour.'

The dragon seemed content with this; in fact, at the mention of Merlin his face seemed to soften somewhat.

'Only the very brave or very stupid would wake a dragon in the dead of winter,' Emrys said, smoke from his nose wreathing around them and his eyes fixed unblinkingly on their faces. 'Which are you?'

'Ah... Er... we're the very desperate,' Bronwyn broke in, trying not to choke. 'This was actually Cerys's idea,' she continued, pushing her sister forward. 'I didn't know you were even here.'

Bronwyn shifted her weight from one leg to the

other, a sure sign of nervousness, and gently put the vases she was still holding back on the pile at her feet.

'So sorry; I hope I haven't damaged anything.'

'We'll let you decide which we are,' Cerys spoke firmly and looked the dragon full in the face without so much as a tremor in her voice. 'Emrys, we're here to ask for your help. Please, Sir. The snow is so thick that the flocks are buried and we're not able to rescue them all in time. Many will die without your help.'

'My help?' The dragon would have raised his eyebrows if he'd had any. 'What am I supposed to do?'

'We need your fire.' Cerys was brief and to the point.

'We do?' Bronwyn swivelled her eyes to her sister in amazement. Had Cerys gone mad?

'The snow must be melted quickly so we can find all the sheep, BUT...,' she paused for effect, 'you are not allowed to roast them or eat them.'

The dragon turned his face away as if he was no longer interested.

'If you do this for us,' Cerys implored, 'we will be beholden to you and will make sure you are not without food when you wake for the summer. As long as we live, I promise you.'

Emrys turned his head back towards them and he certainly looked as though he was thinking about it for a moment, but then slumped back down on his golden pile showering the girls with riches, some of which were sharp but fortunately, bounced off all their layers of clothing.

'Why?' he asked simply, 'Why should I help you?'

It was the question Cerys had dreaded.

'Because... because you're different from the other dragons; not just your handsome colour.' Emrys looked gratified by this compliment. 'You've been here for ever – well, nearly – you've nothing to prove but you love this place; you love Wales and we're the people of Wales; well, some of them anyway. Without the farming folk and the sheep, there would be no Wales; the fields would return to forest, the dragons would die out, our way of life – for all of us – would be lost for ever. I know you've helped people in the past; you helped Merlin all those years ago. Please help us now. Please Emrys; won't you do so again?'

Overcome by emotion, a tear or two trickled down Cerys's cheek as she pleaded for the sake of her father, her family and for Wales.

Emrys, the dragon who had truly once helped the legendary magician Merlin, shifted his weight again and breathed gently into her face, drying her tears and warming her in one short moment.

'Not many people know that story,' he murmured, 'your father must be a remarkable man to have kept that memory alive. I had almost forgotten it myself.'

'So you'll do it?' cried Bronwyn in delight.

The red dragon who had slept in the Glaslyn River Valley for more winters than he could count, nodded slowly.

'I will; for Wales.' Clambering awkwardly to his feet, Emrys gave his instructions. 'Climb on my back children. Let's go'

Now, it is no easy thing to climb onto the back of a dragon and I don't recommend you ever try it. At least not unless you are invited by a dragon of extremely gentle temperament. It was a scramble and a scuffle for the girls but they managed somehow and, with a crunch of coins underfoot, Emrys lumbered his way to the cave mouth where he reared upwards, stretched his wings and in a moment he had left the ground far below. Bronwyn felt her stomach do somersaults and held on more tightly; Cerys savoured the extraordinary sensation of flight. Swooping over the trees – assuming they were still there under the snow – Emrys flew over the Welsh hills, a red streak in a sullen sky.

'There! Down there!' Cerys pointed to the area below them, recognising the farmhouse through the freezing air.

Though her words were snatched in the wind, Emrys must have understood for they felt him take a deep breath in and then, his mouth opened and fire danced across the top of the snow, melting it in a moment, creating instant brooks and rills of ice-cold water. Back and forth he went, never too low, never allowing his fiery breath to penetrate too deep so no sheep would be harmed.

From where they sat, the sisters saw the familiar landmarks of the farm emerge like magic; it was as though a cloth was wiping away everything that wasn't home. There was the tree Bronwyn had climbed to find the bee's honey last summer. Beyond that was the ditch where they had found a helpless sheep on its back two months ago, and there was their mother waving from the farmyard as sheep after sheep emerged from it's enforced trap, shook the melted snow from its fleece and trotted gladly to join the flock, warm itself and share her hot mash.

With a stomach-churning dive, Emrys landed gracefully, depositing the giggling sisters on the ground. They were overjoyed.

'You did it, Emrys! You did it!'

The girls shrieked and cheered as they picked themselves up. There was excitement mixed with relief, jumping and hugging. I must tell you that hugging a dragon is also quite a unique experience. Not many have done so and lived to tell the tale.

But now, their mother was bustling towards them, her face chapped and knitted with anxiety rather than relief. She barely seemed to notice that there was a large, red dragon near the water pump.

'What is it, Ma?' the twins asked together.

'Oh, it's your Da. I don't know where he is. He

hasn't come back. Goodness knows where he's got to.' She wiped her face with the back of her hand and sniffed loudly. 'Oh my; is that all the sheep back? Girls, you're a wonder, that you are. I wish all the farmers were so fortunate.'

'Don't worry,' Cerys reassured her mother. 'Emrys will help us find him.'

Betty looked around to see who her daughter was talking about. 'Oh my stars!' she exclaimed. 'How is that even possible...? A dragon is it? Oh girls...'

But her words faded as once more, with the remarkable sisters on his back, the red dragon of Wales flew again.

'We must find Da quickly,' they shouted, hoping their unusual steed would hear them through the bitterly cold air. 'He must be stuck somewhere.'

Once again Emrys skimmed across the fields. Where the snow was melted by his fire, streams were running to join the river, but there were still many miles of fields covered in the white blanket.

Taking them by surprise now, the dragon lifted his head and made a strange mewing sound. Over and over, the piercing call rang out across the landscape. With a strong flap of wings he gained height, now covering vast distances with a single movement of leathery wings against the crisp air, all the time calling and soaring, swooping and circling.

And then, stranger than all that had happened so far, other sounds were heard on the wind. It was the answering cry of dozens of dragons who had been awakened and summoned by Emrys' call and who now joined him in flight. In the language of dragons he gave commands and immediately they scattered and began to copy what the girls had seen on their own land. Fire-breathing dragons spread across the west of Wales, gently melting the thick snow with their hot breath, birthing streams and releasing sheep from certain death.

All over the hills and valleys, farmers heard the sound of their flocks again and hurried to bring them safely into the fold. It was an astonishing sight. Even if you had been there you would scarcely have believed it.

But now the children's concern for their father had increased so much that they feared for his life. All this snow-melting had taken precious time and the cold can kill a man in less than an hour. Emrys must have felt their anxiety for, breaking off, he returned to their corner of Wales and criss-crossed the ground, his dragon eyes alert for any movement. The girls could barely see anything as the wind rushed past their faces at such speed that their eyelids automatically closed against the force of flight.

Just when all hope seemed lost, Emrys dropped lower and reduced speed, which was quite a relief.

Suddenly, Bronwyn shouted: 'There! Over there;

by the trees!'

'I see something red!' cried Cerys. 'Please let it not be blood!'

The dragon landed again and let the children dismount.

'I don't see him,' Cerys yelled.

'See there!' Bronwyn responded. 'I can see his scarf.'

Sure enough, tangled round some low branches was the scarlet Christmas scarf their mother had made for Idris. On closer investigation, there too was their father, caught in some brambles having lost his footing and fallen while rescuing a sheep. His leg was cut, and the thorns had scratched him badly while holding him tight in their knotty embrace.

With careful help from Emrys, the brambles were burned away, freeing their father at last. There were tears and laughter as the story was told and rejoicing that all the sheep were now safe.

'Thank goodness you wore your scarf, Da!'

'Thank goodness you found a dragon,' replied their father admiringly.

'Not any dragon,' Cerys said with satisfaction as she planted a kiss on the scaly, hot nose of the red dragon of Wales who had once helped Merlin the magician.

And that is how dragons came into their own in the winter of 1740. The sheep and farmers of Wales were saved and they celebrated that Christmas like never before.

Every year Bronwyn and Cerys visited Emrys in the river valley and brought him a brand new hand-knitted scarf to keep him warm during his months of hibernation. He enjoyed the softness and comforting feel of the wool on his neck, but they always got singed and burnt while he snored so heavily through the winter months of hibernation. By the time he woke up each year they had usually disintegrated, consisting of little more than a few unrecognisable black strands, so he was always grateful for a new one, especially if it was red.

The girls grew up, of course, and lived to be very old ladies, and yes, they kept their promise through all those years, taking Emrys his first picnic every spring after his long sleep. They made the happy discovery that their dragon was actually rather bored with the taste of sheep. Luckily they still had the recipe for their mother's porridge-mash which was as nourishing and delicious as any dragon could ever wish for. Emrys always licked the pot clean and much preferred it to sheep.

As far as I know he may sleep still in the Glaslyn River Valley; I was never told. But every time you see the Welsh flag flying, you may wonder too.

THE END

THE END